BABY, COME BACK

M. O'KEEFE

Hey guys!

Thanks so much for picking up Baby, Come Back! I really hope you enjoy it!

Jesse and Charlotte have their own book – Bad Neighbor! You can grab it here:
http://amzn.to/2o4xKAF

Huge thanks to my Facebook Reader Group The Keepers – you are all amazing! Thank you for all the support and the fun over the years.

If you're interested in joining this great group you can find it here:
www.facebook.com/groups/1657059327869189

Abby
BEFORE

I'M NOT SMART about a lot of things, but I know chemistry. Not the stuff in schools, with the beakers and everything; that's a total gong show for me. I didn't even get to Chemistry in high school because I was stuck in freshman Physical Science for four years. Thank God we got a new teacher my senior year, otherwise I never would have passed. Out went Mrs. Baker and in came handsome young Mr. Suarez.

Mr. Suarez did not stand a chance against me.

That he didn't give me an A was probably the thing he clung to at night when the guilt got to be too much for him.

Mr. Suarez was a lesson in *my* kind of chemistry.

The kind that bubbles out of thin air between two particular people. The irresistible attraction that sweeps strangers up in a current, bringing them together despite anything in the way. The kind of chemistry that changes everything.

That's something I understand, down to the ground.

It's my job, really. Or understanding it is what makes me good at my job.

Knowing when someone is looking my way a little bit longer than necessary, and how to manipulate it and feed it and then turn that into money—it's my one skill.

And I'm fucking amazing at it.

Knowing the men to avoid and the women to befriend—it's like a superpower. Chemistry is the secret that turns the world around.

Fuck love.

It's chemistry that gets shit done.

Like an idiot, I thought I knew attraction inside out, from every angle—when you only have one skill, you tend to lean on it pretty hard.

But then I met Jack.

And it wasn't love at first sight—that's for children and idiots. For people who don't fuck their high school science teacher just so they can pass a class.

It wasn't even fear at first sight. That came much later.

But it was chemistry, so much chemistry my whole world blew up.

And me with it.

CHAPTER ONE

Abby

BEFORE

THE GRAY SAN Francisco afternoon vanished as soon as Maria, Sun-hee, and I stepped in through the side door of the Moonlight Lounge. We all had our dresses slung over our shoulders, our makeup bags and hair stuff in suitcase-sized purses clutched in our hands.

I put my stuff down with a groan.

"You gotta pack lighter," Sun muttered.

"Like you're any better?" I asked her, eyeing her duffel bag of stuff.

"It takes work to look this good, girls," Maria said and fished her buzzing phone out of her pocket.

The door closed behind us, shutting us into the dark, silent cave of the empty club.

"Hello? 'Ello? 'Lo?" Sun joked, making her voice echo in the empty room.

"Jeez," Maria said. "It's freezing in here."

The hair on the back of my neck went up and I

wasn't sure if it was cold or just the vibe of the place.

Across from us, on the far side of the room, was an empty stage, the dance floor spread out in front of it. The back wall had doorways and windows leading to what I imagined was the VIP section. The bar was on the other wall; it was all mirror and glass, and when it was lit up it was probably pretty impressive. But without the lights and the people, it looked empty.

It was empty.

Too empty.

"Where is everyone?" Sun asked.

"No idea," I answered. "Are we early?"

"Nope," Maria said, checking the time on her phone. "Six p.m."

"Weird," said Sun.

It was really weird. The bar opened in two hours and the place was completely still and silent. No band setting up. No servers. No sound guy.

And I wasn't very smart about a lot of things, but I was awesome with vibes, and this room was waiting but not in a good way. Other bars we worked in, they were like parties about to happen. Energized and ready. A powder keg needing a spark—and I knew how to be that spark. My whole job was to be that spark.

But I didn't know if I could create a big enough spark to warm up this cold, empty room.

"Look at this place," Maria sighed, looking around

at the shiny silver drapes and the huge chrome modern light fixtures with wide eyes. "It's so classy."

"Classy?" Sun-hee scoffed. Sun scoffed at everything.

"You don't think so? The curtains and stuff?"

"Cheesy," Sun said.

"What do you think, Abby?" Maria asked me, putting me in the standard position of tie-breaker between the two. I did what I always did when we went into a new club: I totally redecorated in my head. I replaced the silver curtains with velvet—something lush, indigo or purple. I replaced the very hip light fixtures with old school chandeliers and built a riser at the edge of the dance floor and put a row of low tables there, covered in white linen with small lamps on top.

Better, I thought, liking the vision in my head. Much warmer.

But the girls I worked with didn't know I did this— they didn't know that I renovated and revamped and reorganized every single bar we worked in, making it better if only in my head.

So I just said:

"I think we're gonna make a shit ton of money."

Predictably, it was the right thing to say, and Maria and Sun high-fived.

"Where is everyone?" I asked, and like I summoned him a voice said, "Ladies!"

We glanced around, looking for the man who belonged to that voice. I found him in the shadows, coming down a set of stairs that led up to the second floor. We watched him make his way toward us.

"Sorry I wasn't here to greet you," the man said, and gave us a little bow. Oh, Maria was going to eat that courtly bow shit right up.

The guy was seriously good-looking in a cold and perfect way. When my sister and I were kids, we had a Ken doll that looked like him: blonde hair, light blue eyes, slight build but tall. He looked pretty slick in his black suit and black tie.

But there was something strange about all his beauty.

He was young, too. Our age, even. But he seemed older.

And it wasn't just that he didn't *look at us*, look at us.

His gaze was vacant. He looked through us. Past us. Into the space we were occupying like he was waiting for us to be gone.

"We're from Elegance Hospitality," I said, because Sun and Maria were just staring at the guy. "Are you Mr....Lazarus?"

That was weird, too, right? Lazarus? Like the guy from the Bible who rose from the dead?

This place was starting to give me the creeps.

"No. Mr. Lazarus is in meetings." He gestured lightly over his shoulder toward the stairs and the windows that made up one whole wall of the second floor. Sun, Maria, and I all looked up at that wide-open eye of a window. It was black so we couldn't see in.

People were watching us. Which was nothing new. People watching us was kind of the point, but a chill went down my spine all the same.

Whoever was watching us did not want us to see them.

And that window was so big, like we were on stage for them.

Creeeepy.

"I will show you to the dressing rooms," the man said. So freaking formal.

"What about the bar and everything?" I asked. "Did the vodka arrive?"

"Patty, when she gets here, will answer those questions. She's our head bartender."

"I didn't catch your name," I said, knowing full well he didn't give it.

"You can call me Bates."

Like a butler? Maybe the guy didn't know it was 2017.

I made the introductions to Maria and Sun. Bates did not shake our hands, only gave us that little head bow again. Out of the corner of my eye I watched Sun and Maria exchange glances.

Weird.

"You guys open at eight, right?" I asked. "Where is everyone?"

He looked around as if he was as surprised as we were to see no one was there. "We're a new club and we don't quite have all the kinks worked out," he said.

"Are you the manager?" I asked.

"No. But you can ask me anything you need. Patty can help you, too."

"Great," I said, but I wasn't sure I meant it. Bars and clubs worked only if management was on freaking point. Without good management, the place could be cool as fuck and full of beautiful people but it wouldn't last.

"Follow me?" Bates said, and because we didn't have a lot of choice, we all followed him across the dance floor.

Three nights. That's all. We could do just about anything for three nights.

And the club wasn't as empty as I thought it was.

One man sat at the shadowy far corner of the bar.

There was a book open in front of him and I watched as he quietly turned the page. The sound of paper sliding across paper was loud in the empty room.

The dude was reading. In a bar.

It was so out of the ordinary I stopped and watched

him. Gawked really, like he was an exhibit in a museum.

He must have felt my attention because he lifted those eyes away from the book and caught me staring.

I couldn't see him well in the shadows, but what I did see was attractive. Dark hair, dark eyes. A lean body with wide shoulders dressed well in a gray suit, a clean white shirt underneath it.

He was tall, filling up that bar stool like he owned it. And very very still.

Interest prickled under my skin.

Hello, handsome.

His gaze made its way over me, from my hair to my feet, and when he got to my beat-up Converse he smiled. Smirked really, and his dark face transformed into something else.

Something I wanted a closer look at.

Compelled by that smirk, I stepped forward and, still smirking, he looked up at my face.

So I did what I always did when a hot mysterious guy smiled at me like that: I flipped my hair, the straight white-blonde sheet of it, over my shoulder and gave him my best "come see about me" look.

It was proven effective, my look.

But Reader took one look at my smile and my hair and my eyes, and the smile fell from his face like it had never been there. In its absence his face was perfectly and completely blank.

Like he'd never smiled before. Ever. Much less at me.

And then he turned around, back to his book.

Ignoring me.

My jaw fell open for one second.

Men, as a rule, did not ignore me. They might not like me. They might think shit things about me, but they did not ignore me.

"You coming?" Sun yelled across the empty bar.

"Yeah."

Whatever, I thought as I followed my friends through the doors to the dressing room. *What was I going to do with a guy who reads books in a bar?*

Nothing, was the answer. I was going to do nothing with that guy.

"I LOVE THIS place," Sun-hee said a half hour later as we sat in front of the big mirrors in the dressing room. "I love these dressing rooms. I love that stage..." She looked at me in the mirror as we put on our false eyelashes. "I'm going to be on that stage, mark my words."

"I believe you," Maria said.

Sun was making a name for herself in the music scene and she wouldn't be working for Elegance for very long. We all knew that. And Maria was looking for another job—she and her husband just had a baby and she wanted something with better hours.

"Look at my sweet girl," Maria cooed, flipping her phone around to show us a picture her husband had taken of their baby sleeping in a crib. Sun rolled her eyes but I took the phone and looked closely.

"She's sitting up now, did I tell you?" Maria asked. "All by herself."

"She's so beautiful," I said, so deeply envious I could barely stand it. Not just of the baby and the husband—which were pretty enviable things—but all of it.

Sun-hee and Maria had futures. They had *plans*.

Maria had a freaking *home*. A baby to love and spoil and a husband to love and spoil her. And Sun had all this ambition, like a path set out in front of her that she was so determined to see through.

I had… a bag of cosmetics. A growing savings account. A dream I never talked about. And an empty apartment.

Oh, and my sister.

I loved Charlotte, but she wasn't keeping me warm at night, you know?

After Moonlight Lounge I was only moving on to the next club. And the next club after that. A different booze, a different outfit, same job.

I was putting money aside for this gigantic dream I

had, but some days… most days actually, the dream seemed ridiculous. Like what was a person like me doing, dreaming a dream like the one I had? I barely had a high school diploma. I was a glorified fucking shots girl.

I couldn't even say my dream out loud or really look directly at it. It was embarrassing to want something so big, you know?

Which was stupid, but I was known to be stupid

"So what are we doing tonight?" Maria asked when I reluctantly handed back the phone and the picture of her daughter. Maria was looking at me. Sun looked, too.

Honest to God, I didn't understand why I was the one making these decisions. Maria had been a part of the company the longest and Sun had the bigger personality, but it didn't seem to matter.

At some point I had been voted leader.

"I'll work the floor, Maria you work VIP, and Sun will float," I said. "Check in at midnight and switch if we need to?"

"Works for me," Sun said. Maria nodded and it was decided.

I was wearing my hair in a classic twist and keeping my makeup real retro, a look that went with the outfits and the club. The lights around the mirror were reflected in my pupils and it looked like I had empty golden eyes.

"That blonde guy creeped me out," Maria said.

Sun laughed, low in her throat. "You know what all these guys do, right?" she whispered.

"What?" Maria asked, looking up from her phone all wide-eyed.

"They're like gangsters. Mobsters," Sun whispered. "Lazarus is like one of the biggest drug traffickers in the whole Bay area. I heard he traffics women, too."

"No!" Maria said, all incredulous. "That's just the vibe of the club. It's not real."

Sun laughed. "It's totally real. My cousin told me. Watch them—"

"Shhhhh!" I shushed everyone, because real or not it wasn't something we needed to be talking about while in the dressing rooms.

"You don't believe me?" Sun asked, because she could not let anything go.

"No. And you need to stop talking about it," I whispered, glancing around.

Sun shook her head at me like I was something to be pitied.

"There's a guy at the bar reading, Sun. Does that seem very gangster to you?"

"I think you got a thing for the guy at the bar."

"What are you talking about?" I needlessly swept more mascara over my eyelashes. "I didn't say two words to him."

"No, but you gave him your *come get in my pants* look and he did not take the bait."

Maria laughed and I tried to scowl, but Sun jostled me with her shoulder and in the end I smiled. "Totally struck out," I said with a laugh. "But I don't think he's a gangster."

I didn't want this place to be filled with gangsters. I didn't want The Reader to be a bad guy.

I'd learned my lesson with the bad guys.

My first boyfriend, which probably told you everything you needed to know about my instincts, gave me a black eye.

I liked the grumpy guys, who gave their smiles only to me and weren't super excited to meet my friends, but would do it because they loved me.

The assholes with temper issues and inferiority complexes were not for me.

That was another skill I had developed over the years: differentiating the harmless grumpy guys from the asshole grumpy guys. I was so good at it I could smell it on them.

Reader wasn't one of the bad ones.

I was *mostly* sure of it.

The door opened and a beautiful black woman with dreadlocks, who wore a man's vest and cigarette pants, poked her head in the door.

"I'm Patty," she said with a tight smile. "The bar-tender. You guys good in here?"

"Fine," I said.

"Your vodka arrived. When you're done let's get things organized."

"Sounds good," I said and Patty vanished.

Caprice Vodka was paying Elegance a stupid amount of money for us to come into this bar, dress up in their custom costume, and give away their over-priced potato juice. Introduce people to the product, make the first experience so amazing they had to come back for more. It wasn't a hard job. Not when you looked like the three of us.

"You guys need a little party-starter?" Sun asked, taking out the small amber bottle of coke she had tucked in her bra. She did a bump and so did Maria, but I shook my head.

"No thanks."

The vibe of this place made me feel like someone needed to be clear-headed tonight.

"Suit yourself," Maria said and put her feet in her high-heeled leather booties, fluffed her skirt, and headed out to the bar. Sun followed, fierce and glittering.

In our costumes we looked like old school cigarette girls, with sparkly short dresses, puffed out by itchy netting. We wore black hose with the seam up the back and we carried little boxes with straps around our necks, but instead of smokes we sold shots.

But really we sold a feeling.

My sister didn't understand. She said she did, but I knew deep down she thought I was a glorified stripper or a high-end prostitute.

But I wasn't either of those things.

I was a party starter. A human version of what Sun had in her bra. And I got paid well to do it.

I gave myself one more second in front of the mirror to put on my lipstick. A bright red that made my eyes bluer, my hair brighter.

I looked hot in this dress. My makeup was perfection. My hair, too. This was me. I had this shit in the bag. And the men staring at me to prove it. To remind me. To show me, when I wasn't sure or I forgot, who I was. What my value was.

And if that made me sad? If I wanted *more*?

The baby and the husband and the future and my dream.

I'd get over it.

I'd adapt.

I'd start the party.

It was what I was good at.

CHAPTER TWO

Abby

BEFORE

THE READER DID work for the club. He was security at the bottom of the stairs that led up to the big dark window and the second story. He stood there, with his legs braced wide and his arms over his chest like some kind of pirate. A silent, watching warrior.

Except the only thing he seemed to be watching was me.

But only when my back was turned.

His gaze was a heavy, weighty thing over my hair and back, the side of my face, even my legs.

But when I turned, my neck prickling, he would just be scanning the crowd, like a security guy doing his job.

The first hour of this, I thought I was imagining it. I mean, his job was to watch the crowd, and I was in fact part of the crowd. It was inevitable he'd glance over me from time to time, and it was my own overactive self-worth that thought he was looking at me.

But as the night wore on he got sloppy, and I kept catching him like Billy Hauser in eighth grade. Looking away too fast when I caught him looking at me.

It was actually kind of cute.

And considering his beautiful face and long lanky body in that fine suit—it quickly got hot.

Not interested on my part became *totally fucking interested.*

When I watched him through my eyelashes he really looked the part of a gangster. Dressed sharp and giving the impression of something deadly all the same. His blank face still and composed, giving away nothing but the slight whiff of disdain. I watched him turn everyone away from that stairwell with just a shake of his head.

But he was just a bouncer in character for this club. It was a clever bit of staging, just like me.

He looked gangster, but he wasn't really.

As the night wore on, this little game of his was all I could feel. Not the pinch of my shoes or the ache of the cocktail box around my neck. The trickle of sweat down my spine.

Just the hot slide of his eyes over me every few minutes.

I circled the small cocktail tables while Sun and

Maria worked the back VIP rooms. Bottle service was flying out the door and we were all grinning at each other.

Our cash bags were stuffed.

I poured out shots for a couple sitting in the big banquettes at the back of the room and felt my neck tingle in a way that had become familiar.

The Reader.

Again.

Turning, I caught his eyes for a second before he glanced away, scanning the room like a man who was just doing his job.

Oh, he did not know the trouble he was starting.

Give me a man pretending not to be interested and I'd turn myself inside out to get him to stop pretending.

I wanted to smile and go pet his slicked-back hair, mess it up.

He could look all he liked—that was the point of me. The point of the dress and the silk stockings. I would tell him I liked him looking at me.

And I really liked him smiling at me.

Fuck it, I thought and I made my way over to his side.

"You need anything?" I asked above the sound of the crowd and the band.

He shook his head.

"A drink or whatever?"

Still he didn't look at me. He kept scanning the crowd like I wasn't there.

"Who do you think you're kidding?" I asked with a laugh that finally got his attention. "Yeah," I said. "You've been staring at me all night."

He looked at me again, a sly second, a bright moment and I felt the shimmy of interest, the cat curl of desire.

Oh, you man, you don't know it yet. But you are mine.

"Part of my job," he said, pretending that there was something more interesting than me happening over my shoulder when we both knew that there wasn't.

But I liked the show of it, the game.

"Watching me is part of your job?"

"Watching everyone." Oh, he was telling me I wasn't special. Except I was. I was pretty fucking special.

"Your loss," I said and walked back into the crowd to do my job.

Trouble, a voice whispered in my head. A voice that sounded very much like my sister's. *This man is trouble and you know it. You feel it.*

But wasn't that the problem?

I loved trouble.

SUN, MARIA AND I all arrived together on the second night too, a little trick that we'd learned about traveling in a group. The bars we went to were upscale places, they had to be to afford us, but upscale had its own kind of creep.

And when we were together no one bothered us. We had a hard glittering asshole-repellent force field that I think actually came mostly from Sun, but whatever, I'd travel under her force field any day.

The side door closed behind us and we all stood there for a second, blinking in the dim light. Bates didn't come running to greet us and Patty wasn't behind the bar. There was, however, a band setting up on stage.

The band was irrelevant to me.

I searched the shadowy corner of the bar, looking for The Reader. And I couldn't hide my smile when I saw him there, his shoulders bent and though I couldn't see it, I knew he had a book open in front of him.

"You're acting like a whipped little girl. You get that, right?" Sun asked.

"I don't care," I told her. And I didn't.

This was chemistry and it made everything else seem insignificant.

The Reader wasn't wearing his jacket, and the fine white fabric of his shirt pulled taut across his shoulders, and all I wanted was to run my hand over that shoulder. Feel the heat of his skin through the cotton.

His hair wasn't pushed off his forehead, held in place by some gross gel. It was slipping into his eyes and it was curly. Really curly.

Wavy and thick and completely irresistible.

The hair made me do it, really. His hair freaking compelled me.

"You coming?" Sun asked, standing in the middle of the dance floor looking back at me because I hadn't moved from the doorway.

"Give me a second."

Sun shook her head. "Look at you, so hot for a man just because he's not hot for you."

"Fuck off, Sun," I said. Because he was hot for me, he just—for some soon-to-be-inconsequential reason—wasn't ready to admit it yet.

I walked toward the bar where The Reader sat turning pages, a cup of coffee at his elbow. His sleeves were rolled up, revealing thick forearms covered in tattoos.

Oh. Sweet. Lord.

Really, he was all of my favorite things.

He swept back the dark curls from hanging in his eyes so he could keep reading. The move reminded me so much of my sister that it made him seem safe. Familiar.

I should have known better.

"Hey," I said, leaning against the bar, close enough he could smell my perfume.

He glanced up and then back down at his book. "Dressing room is through the far door."

"I know." I tilted my head so my hair fell down across my shoulder, pooling just a little left of his hand. I saw his fingers twitch and tried not to smile.

"You need something?" he asked, turning the page.

"Just thought I'd say hi. Be friendly."

He glanced up and his eyes were dark blue. Like navy. The color of twilight or the ocean on a dark day. They were made more beautiful by the thick lashes they were surrounded by. He had dark caramelly skin, a firm jaw, and a nose that looked like it had been broken once.

And that fucking hair.

"I'm Abigail," I said, holding out my hand.

He glanced at my hand and then back at his book. And as a dismissal it might have worked if he hadn't spent five hours last night tracking me across this bar, like I was a deer he was hunting.

"People call me Abby."

He nodded as if that made sense, like he'd been taking bets on what my name was and that worked out just fine for him.

"Sooo," I drawled when he was silent. "Usually what happens next is you tell me your name."

"That's what happens next?" Those deep ocean eyes of his had a twinkle, just a flash and then gone.

"Usually."

"Jack."

"Nice to meet you, Jack."

He was silent.

"What are you reading?"

That made him look up again with what I could have sworn was hope on his face, like a dog when you walk by his leash.

But then he looked back down, ignoring me.

Fuck, this guy was tough. But the tough ones were worth it. I peeked over his shoulder at the title on the top of the page.

"*Tipping Point*," I cried. "I read that." Inwardly I cringed at my own eagerness. Not at all cool. But there were not that many books I could say that about. And what were the chances he was reading one of those few books I had managed to finish?

Silent, he looked up at me. Clearly a man of few words, but again, his attention felt like interest. Like he didn't just hand that out to everyone.

"Well, I listened to it," I qualified. "Audiobook at the gym." And yes, mentioning the gym had the predictable effect of making him look down at me, scanning my body in a quick second as if confirming— yep, I was in killer shape. "My sister wouldn't shut up about it a few Christmases ago, and I listened to it so we could talk about it. It's good, right? You liking it?"

I swallowed back a few more far-too-eager words and had the very foreign feeling of having said too much. It was the book talk—threw me off my game.

"I read it a few years ago," he said, his voice a quiet thing. A careful thing. Like he didn't use it a whole lot. "I'm re-reading."

"Small things can make big changes," I said, quoting the book.

His lip turned up for just a moment and I was struck by how elegant he was. Thin and sharp, the dress shirt cut just right over his shoulders.

And his silence was like a magnet, pulling out all of my words.

"I started to put some of it to work with my job, and you'd be amazed at how much more booze I sell. People really respond to some of that stuff. And once I started like really paying attention and trying to capitalize on those small things, I could see it working all over the place."

There was a moment of silence after my rush of excited words and I heard my own voice, my own stupid eagerness.

Selling booze? Good God, Abby!

My face got painfully hot and my skin itched like a rash and I realized I was blushing. Something I hadn't done in years. Since I was a kid standing up in class with the wrong answer to the wrong question.

Wrong, always wrong.

Guys I was usually interested in did not talk about books, and here I was four minutes into a conversation and I was out of my depth.

"That sounds dumb." I took a step back, aborting project The Reader

"It doesn't sound dumb at all."

"I mean, I know he wasn't talking about selling booze—"

"It's not dumb," he insisted. "It's very smart."

I gaped at him because the truth was, no one ever— and I mean EVER—accused me of being smart.

And I felt myself opening up, blinking like I couldn't believe my eyes. What a strange conversation, like one of the strangest in my life. I talked about a book. He called me smart. I had no idea what to do next.

This wasn't my usual brand of chemistry. There was something unpredictable about it, something I couldn't manipulate, and its hooks were sunk deep inside of me. I waited for him to say more, but he didn't.

"You don't talk a lot, do you?" I asked.

"You talk plenty for both of us." Again he smiled, and I was ruined by that smile. Torn to pieces by that smile, by the implied intimacy of his words.

"You want to get a drink after work?" I asked, because that was usually the next step in this dance.

The smile fell from his face and I was flooded by the strange sensation of having gotten this all wrong.

Like, the Reader didn't want me after all.

"You don't want to get a drink after work," he said, his voice low and warm. Intimate.

Ah, this was slightly more familiar.

"I don't?" I said, giving him the coyest of my coy smiles. "What do I want?"

"You want me to take you back to my place."

The heat between us was thick. Humid.

"You're jumping ahead a few steps, aren't you?" I asked.

I'd tipped my head and didn't realize that my hair was now touching his hand until he opened his palm. We both watched as he took the ends of my hair and rubbed them between his thumb and forefinger.

The way someone would touch velvet or silk; as if to see if it was as soft as it looked.

I couldn't feel it, I knew that, my hair was dead and he wasn't exerting any force, I felt no sting in my scalp of him pulling it.

But I felt something.

I felt something so big it changed the beat of my heart.

"You're very beautiful," he said. I was silent, all my energy on breathing and my hair and watching him twine it between his fingers. "But you know that."

I did. I knew that. It was the prevailing truth of my life. But he made it sound sad. Like my beauty was a thing that hurt him.

"Last night, I couldn't take my eyes off you."

"You said you weren't watching me."

He smiled, lightning quick, there and gone.

"We both know I was lying."

I could not help but lean forward, everything about him—his face, his eyes, the soft whisper of his voice—compelling me closer. And closer.

He curled his hand into a fist around my hair, finally pulling it, the fine threads stinging at my scalp. The pain so welcome I nearly moaned, shocked. But my shock was laced with heat, a kind of back splash of desire. I felt flooded with adrenaline and connection.

He leaned forward, speaking right into my ear, his breath sending chills down my spine.

"This place is not for you," he said, and his low voice contained an edge. A warning. A threat?

"What are you talking about?" I tried to lean back, away from him so I could see his eyes, but his hand was a sudden fist in my hair, holding me still. Hurting... just a little.

Fear curled through me. Fear, desire, the great

velvety depth of the unknown between us.

He leaned forward, his knee pressing into me between my legs, and I bit my lip, swallowing back a whimper. His eyes were fixated on my lips like he was memorizing them. Like there might be a test later.

"Don't pretend, princess. You felt it when you walked in yesterday. I saw it on your face."

I couldn't argue, so I didn't bother. Instead, I pushed just slightly against his knee, feeling in this dark bar, like an animal. Like we were both just animals.

Despite the fear.

Because of the fear?

I didn't know anymore.

"This is a warning," he said. "Keep your head down. Stop talking to me and don't think about anything but leaving."

"I shouldn't think about you?"

He pulled again on my hair, like his fingers twitched out of his control. "This isn't a game, princess. I don't exist for you. And you don't exist for me. Not even a little."

He let go of my hair and sat back, his face completely blank, like nothing had happened between us. Like I was a stranger asking for directions.

It was utterly disorienting, considering I was panting and nearly sweating and so fucking turned on my body was giving off sparks.

Cold and unruffled, he turned back to his book.

All at once I felt dumb. Like I'd imagined the last few minutes. And dumb did not sit well with me—I'd had my fill of that when I was a kid.

"If you have problems, you can talk to Patty," he said, as I stood there seething. "You should move on, I'm busy."

I waited a second for him to do something. Say something. Call me princess. Ask me nicely. Anything. But he kept turning pages like I wasn't even there.

And the thing about me, mostly because I really wasn't very smart, is that I never said the right thing at the right time. Like it was always two days later, standing in the shower, that I figured out what I should have said to some asshole in line at the grocery store.

And with Jack? My brain had been fried.

"Fuck you" was pretty much the best I could come up with and I walked off, hair swinging, chin high.

This time I didn't feel his eyes on me. And I was cold through and through.

CHAPTER THREE

Abby

BEFORE

I HAD SETTLED into ignoring him when he left.

Which was hours ago. Just after the doors opened and the band started up, Bates went over and whispered something in Jack's ear, and Jack and another guy headed toward the side door.

At that moment, Jack's face had not been carefully blank. He'd been scowling. His cheeks red with what looked like anger. He'd looked... terrifying. A well-dressed wild man.

But just before he walked out the door he turned around and found me in the crowd, staring at him.

And he stared right back. For one long, hot second. He pinned me in place with his eyes. With his attention. I couldn't move. I could barely breathe.

He shouldn't go, I thought with something that felt like panic. Whatever he was leaving for... it wasn't going to be good.

I took a step toward him, and he shook his head at me. Just once. A short sharp *don't*.

And then he was gone.

I wanted to not give a shit. But he walked out of the club and he took something with him. That delicious chemical in the air, the glitter and the foreplay of his eyes watching me.

And now, despite the killer band and the money I was making, I was off my game. I poured shots and I smiled and I delivered bottles to the VIP's, but my head was distracted.

Stop, I told myself. *Stop. He's… too intense. I am not made for intensity. I am made for good times. For parties and fun. Casual and flirty.*

He was like midnight in the middle of the day. A dark cloud that sucked in everything.

So I told myself I was relieved he was gone, with his constant watching and his warnings, but I kept checking the doors waiting for him to come back.

Because really what I was, was worried.

Around midnight I was circling the edge of the dance floor, where people were standing, listening to the band, mopping off sweaty foreheads, guzzling booze like it was water when behind me the side door suddenly opened.

A blast of wet cold San Francisco air rippled over us and we all turned.

Jack.

He stormed in, smelling like rain and metal, his face a thundercloud, his body an electric current as he walked past me, so close I could feel the damp on his overcoat. He bypassed the coat check and the bar, walking through the club while the guy who came in with him ran up the stairs to the second floor like someone was chasing him.

Jack's blue eyes found me in the dark and restless crowd and it was like tripping, but catching myself before I fell, like hitting the brakes just in time. A panic and a relief all at once.

Jack wasn't that big, but walking across the bar, he was huge. He was larger than life. People instinctively got out of his way and as he passed them they followed him with their eyes. Worried almost that having been that close to him was a bad thing. Like he was a shadow they could not shake off.

The Grim Reaper.

A horseman of the apocalypse.

And I wanted him so badly I had to lock my knees.

He slammed through the doors that led back to the dressing rooms and a staff bathroom. I glanced up at Sun, who with one look at my face rolled her eyes and mouthed "go" at me.

That was all the encouragement I needed. I shoved my way through the crush around the dance floor, and once the staff door closed behind me the band was muffled and the sound of the crowd was distant. But the silence of these private rooms—it was ominous and it pounded in my ears, along with my hard-beating heart. I set down my drink tray and walked down the long hallway, past the band's greenroom toward the bathroom.

I could hear running water. The consistent and persistent mutter of someone talking under their breath.

"Hello?" My voice was some shaky nervous thing and I wondered where all my bravado from earlier today had gone. To say nothing of my resolve not to care about this guy.

I was here. And I was nervous. And I cared.

The door to the bathroom was open and there was Jack, at the sink, his sleeves rolled up his forearms.

The tattoos on his arms were beautiful. Bright and colorful, but full of terrible horrible images of bloody deaths and avenging angels. His tattoos looked like stained glass windows from church, heavy on bloody swords and crying women.

So incredible were the tattoos that it took me a second to realize most of them were splattered in blood. Real blood. It was across his chest and a wide arc of it was dotting his face.

And he was the one talking under his breath. I

caught the words: *Forgive me, Father, for I have sinned.*

Oh Jesus.

He was *praying.*

Mistake, this is a mistake.

Even as I thought it, even as I *knew* it, I didn't move. I couldn't. I wasn't sure if it was the blood or the prayers that kept me there. Or just the magnet at his core that I could not resist.

Perhaps I made a noise, some raw sound from my throat, or maybe he saw me from the corner of his eye. I didn't know but he turned and his eyes, the blue of them, they burned and I was pinned to the spot. My knees suddenly shaking.

"What are you doing?" he asked, his voice a growl. He stepped out of the bathroom, looking up and down the empty hallway. "Why are you here?"

"You're... I was worried."

"You shouldn't be here."

"You... You're praying." It was the wrong thing to say. So the wrong thing. But everything was upside down. He stepped toward me and too late I realized what a mistake I'd made. Everything I'd done with him was a mistake. When he looked up from that bar yesterday I should have looked away. I should have turned around and ignored him. I should have listened to every instinct that said he wasn't for me.

Dumb. Dumb. Dumb.

I turned as if to leave, wanting to leave, but he grabbed my arm, his touch so searing I gasped.

"Do you think this is a joke?" he asked, and I shook my head so fast my earrings slapped my face. "A game maybe?"

"No."

"You're lying. I'm just a thing you want because I don't want you."

I found some feeble bravery left in my shaking body and I turned to look at him, his eyes the color of night, his face flushed and splattered with blood.

Oh my god, what am I doing, I thought even as I said:

"Now who is lying?"

He wanted me as much as I wanted him. His desire was in his face. His eyes. His voice. It was in the way he touched me. I tasted it across my tongue every time I inhaled.

His thumb stroked the inside of my elbow and a sound came out of my throat I could not control. He heard it and the rough timbre of his laughter tickled down my spine, across the nape of my neck, sending goose bumps over my entire body.

"This is why you watch me? Why you came back here? You want to be scared?" he asked. "Hurt?"

"No," I said.

"Don't lie."

"I'm not."

He scoffed and pushed me away. "Get out of here."

And because I wasn't smart like my sister, and because he was so much of all my favorite things, and because the chemistry in my body responding to the chemistry in his was literally the most powerful thing I'd ever felt for another person, I didn't run.

I turned toward him.

He was breathing hard and his cheeks were flushed like it was everything he could do to keep himself under control.

And all I wanted was for him to break.

I put my hand against his chest, the fine white fabric of his shirt, the skin beneath it hotter even than I had imagined it to be.

At my touch he hissed.

I found a whole lot of courage in that reaction.

So I lifted my shaking hand and my fingertip, the long edge of my nail, touched a spot of blood on his chin and another on his cheek. And another near his eye. Connecting the dots like cities on a map.

"Are you hurt?" I whispered.

"No."

"The blood—"

"Not mine."

Later I would think about it, wonder how I'd been so brave. So bold, but I cupped his face in my hand, the rough scrape of his day-old beard against my palm echoing around my body. Like I was a bell for him to ring.

"What do you want?" he asked, baffled.

"You."

"Like this?" His voice broke like the idea was impossible, that a woman would want him blood-splattered and praying in a club bathroom.

"Like this."

"You don't know me. You don't know anything about me."

"So," I breathed, "show me."

And he broke.

He broke so hard. So perfectly. He put his hands at my waist and took one step forward, pushing me back against the hallway, lifting me up off my feet. I was hung there suspended by his strength, and then the hard press of his body against mine.

And then his mouth. His kiss.

Whatever I expected from this man's kiss… it was not what I got. It was not punishing or mean. He was not stamping me or claiming me. It was not the kiss of a man with something to prove.

It was gentle. Soft.

It was the kiss of a man with something he needed forgiven.

He kissed me like absolution was in my body.

And that—in my long life of kissing—was completely new. Totally different.

I melted against him. My arms around his neck, my legs coming up around his waist.

I felt him hard against me and I was soft and wet in welcome. My edges loose, my boundaries gone, dissolved into nothing under this man's cautious kiss.

A surprise. What a fucking surprise he was.

We kissed like that, softly, sweetly, for minutes and I could have done it for hours. Days.

"Jack." Bates's voice rang out and Jack jerked against me as if a shot had gone off. For one second I felt this incredible tension in his body, and I wondered, slightly hysterically, if he was about to take off running down the hallway away from Bates. With me in his arms.

Yes, I wanted to whisper in his ear.

Do it, I wanted to say against his skin.

Take us away from here.

But I kept my mouth shut, because that would be fucking crazy and I'd already slipped in over my head with this man. Finally, as if forcing his muscles back under his control, Jack stepped back. Away from me. My legs fell from around his waist and my hands from around his neck. Until all that connected us was his hand at my stomach, as if to be sure I wouldn't fall over. I was grateful for that, happy for that, because I wasn't sure of my own knees. Or my ankles in my shoes.

Or my heart inside my skin.

"You're needed upstairs," Bates said, his voice the coldest thing I'd ever heard, so cold I actually flinched. I glanced over Jack's shoulder and saw Bates's perfect face staring back at me. He appeared no different than he always did—he even managed to give me a slight, tight-lipped smile edged in ice.

And I had the very real fear that I'd gotten Jack in trouble.

Serious trouble.

"One second, Bates," Jack said, his face still turned toward me but his eyes cast down, away like he knew better than to look at me.

After a long terrifying moment Bates left and I exhaled a breath, leaning back against the wall. Jack's hand left my stomach but I could still feel the imprint of it there. I put my hand where his had been as if I could hold the feeling there. Cup it against me. Protect it from the chill.

"Is he your boss or something?" I asked.

"Something," he said, and then he ran his hands over his face, rubbing at his eyes. "Look… this was a mistake."

"You don't believe that." He'd been hard against me; I still felt him on my body. I would, undoubtedly, for days. If I were to reach forward and touch the zipper of his black dress pants, I was sure he'd still be hard.

This time when he looked at me it was with terrible scorn. So much scorn I flinched.

"Look at you," he sneered. "All you have to do is snap your fingers and the world is brought to your heels—"

"That's not—"

"I'm not a prize."

"I am," I said, my chin up.

For a moment I thought he might smile. I even smiled at him to encourage it, but then he shook his head.

"Forget what happened here," he said.

"Impossible," I said. "And I don't think you're going to forget about me, either. I think you're going to go home tonight and think about me until you can't stand—"

He leaned forward, pressing his forehead against mine, hard, like he wanted to push his words into my skull.

"Do you know who I am?" he groaned. "Do you know what I do here?"

I was silent, because I couldn't pretend anymore that he just dressed the part.

He was still covered in blood.

Oh God.

I leaned back suddenly, realizing that I would have blood on my skin now too. I touched my face as if I could feel it and my face… my face must have told him something about my horror.

His thumb brushed over my cheek. The edge of my nose.

"You're fine," he said, "Clean."

He was a bad man. A bad, bad man. And he did bad things. And I would be a fool to still want him.

An idiot.

"Stay away from me," he said. "Please."

And then he was down the hallway, unrolling the sleeves of his white shirt. The bloody biblical tattoos vanishing under the fine fabric.

And I still wanted him.

CHAPTER FOUR

Abby

BEFORE

MY TWIN'S NAME is Charlotte, and there's a picture on the wall in my parents' condo in Florida that completely encapsulates our entire childhood.

I think it's from our seventh birthday, and Mom made one of those cakes with the doll in it, so the cake looks like her dress? Anyway, me and Charlotte were apeshit over that cake. Mom frosted half of it in yellow for Charlotte and half in pink for me.

In the picture Charlotte's about four inches taller than me, so much taller in fact that she looks like my older sister and not my twin.

Charlotte's got her arm around me, and she's smiling so hard at the camera her eyes have disappeared. Her crazy curly hair is in pigtails and she's pretty much happiness brought to life.

I'm standing next to her, looking two years younger than my age, gray-faced, sucking on an inhaler and giving everyone my best young side-eye.

My family used to make these jokes about how Charlotte starved me out in the womb, and they were stupid crappy jokes that hurt Charlotte so I never made them and I'd yell at anyone who did.

But somehow those jokes got woven into our relationship. Charlotte took care of me like it was her job, like she was apologizing for her health in the face of my un-health. Everywhere we went, she made sure I had my inhaler and my EpiPen. She helped me with homework, and if we went over to someone's house after school she'd be the one asking if there was a cat or dog in the house. And if there was, she'd be the one explaining why we couldn't go in.

And then she'd walk home with me like she didn't care that we didn't have friends.

She acted like I was all she needed, and I think I acted the same way. We were an inseparable force for a long time.

But I was pissed.

I had to be the angriest kid at Lincoln Elementary School.

I was angry because I didn't have any friends and I couldn't go over to anyone's house because everyone had a pet, and my report cards were full of D's when hers were full of A's.

And that I had to work so freaking hard for those

D's.

And I'm not proud of this, and I didn't blame my sister, but I took it out on her. I took it out on her because she was there. Because she looked at me with pity in her eyes.

When someone projects a constant "I'm so sorry" onto you, well, you can grow a pretty serious "fuck you" response.

Anyway, for years I thought this was just the way we would be, Charlotte and me. Her taking care of me. Her helping me with school, with jobs, with my life.

And my resentment—oh God, it burned. It burned so hot inside me I would lie in my single bed across the room from her single bed and I would think I would die I resented her so much.

And then something miraculous happened.

Puberty.

I outgrew my asthma. Most of my allergies.

I got boobs. Great boobs. Hips. Great hips. My hair got long and shiny and my face changed and my voice changed, and suddenly instead of feeling powerless, I felt all kinds of power.

The way boys looked at me gave me power. The way girls looked at me gave me another kind of power.

Charlotte got the pimples and she gained weight that she never lost and she retreated deep inside her brilliant, creative head.

And I was—for the first time in my life—living out loud in my body.

I only graduated high school because Charlotte pretty much dragged me through, and while she was looking at colleges I was looking at studio apartments.

She went on to art school, where she pretty much slayed for four years, and now she's a hot shot designer/illustrator living in a fabulous condo, sometimes forgetting to shower for a few too many days in a row.

I got a job in a bar because I'm hot.

And nothing has changed. Not for years. My life is… one long stretch of the same. Party, bar, party, bar, party, bar.

And when I look at pictures of Maria's baby, I get sick with wishing for something more. When I think about my savings account and that dream I don't ever talk about, I feel so small I can barely move.

And when I think of my sister and her amazing talent I'm filled with something I don't want to name, but feels like hot, hot jealousy.

Charlotte and I meet for dinner a few times a week. I remind her to shower, and that people aren't terrifying wild animals, and she should try to meet a few, and she tells me to pay my taxes and talks me off ledges with men and tries—without much luck—to get me to find a different job.

But I don't resent her anymore, and I hope she

doesn't resent me. Sometimes I catch her looking at me like I'm some kind of creature that wandered in off the street, but I don't think she means it.

I hope she doesn't.

The day after Jack's kiss, though, I felt like a creature that had walked in off the street. I felt not myself, and what was worse—the worst—was I couldn't tell her. I couldn't tell my sister about any of it.

Not just because she would try to convince me to walk away from Jack—which, I could be honest, was sound advice.

But because all of this would stress her out.

And she was already stressed out by me.

She'd made it her life's work to be stressed out by me and I had—for years—made it my job to stress her out.

But I was twenty-four years old. I couldn't punish her for something that wasn't her fault forever.

I let myself into my sister's condo with my key, wondering how I was going to manage not talking about Jack, when all I thought about about was Jack.

"Char?" I yelled.

"I'm in the office!" she cried. "Give me a second."

Right. Charlotte's seconds could be another hour if she was in her office.

"I know I said let's go out, but can we just order in?" I asked, shrugging out of my coat and putting it down on the back of the purple velvet chaise lounge. And then I just collapsed on the chaise lounge. She'd painted flowers on her ceiling, bright red poppies, right above this spot.

That, right there, was so Charlotte.

"You okay?" Charlotte yelled.

"Fine," I said, and I heard the creak of her chair rolling across the floor upstairs.

"Why are you lying?" she yelled.

"Why do you think I'm lying?"

"I know something is wrong when you don't want to go out."

I smiled at the poppies. What incredible medicine to have someone know you so well.

She came downstairs a few seconds later. My sister was a total one of a kind: crazy fashion sense, the same wild white blonde hair, but hers was super curly, where mine was straight as a pin.

Today she wore bright blue leggings and an *I Stand With Standing Rock* tee shirt. She was scowling at me through her red glasses.

"Uh oh," she said.

I figured I looked about how I felt, which was like shit.

"I didn't sleep last night."

"What happened?" she asked.

I shrugged. "Hard to say."

Char walked over and put her hand on my fore-head. She'd been my mother growing up, far more than our own mother, and this, her hand on my forehead, was as familiar as breathing.

"You don't feel hot."

"I'm not sick," I said, taking her hand in mine and giving it a squeeze before letting it go. "But let's figure out dinner, I'm starved."

"Sure. We can get whatever you want."

See? I knew she would say that. Part of our child-hood endlessly playing out.

"Sushi from the place on the corner?"

"Sounds great."

"Can you order?" I asked even though we both had the number in our cells. I could play my part from our childhood too. I wasn't proud of it, but the pattern was fucking seductive.

"Abby!"

"Please?"

She made a show of grumbling, but all the same she walked into the kitchen where her phone was always on the counter. I lay back on her chaise lounge and toed off my boots.

"Extra California rolls!" I shouted.

"Am I not your twin?" she yelled. "Do I not know your sushi order?"

I sighed and melted back against the lounge, thinking, despite my efforts not to, of Jack. His hand against my stomach, the press of his fingers through the dress, as vivid now as it was last night.

She came back into the living room with a bottle of wine and two glasses.

"None for me," I said. "I have to work tonight."

She blinked, because I wasn't averse to a couple drinks before work. Nothing crazy, but like the vial in Sun's dress, it just went with the job.

But I was so off tonight. From last night. And I didn't know how this would end. I worried drinks would make me feel even more out of control.

"Boo," she said, which made me smile.

She sat in the orange chair across from me, folding her legs up under her and opening the wine bottle. She flapped her shirt out around her belly because she was always worrying about her belly. "You want to tell me what's going on? And let's just skip the part when you say *nothing* and I say, *I can tell it's not nothing* and you say—"

"Do you ever want... more?"

She blinked. "More what?"

That wasn't right. I sighed, wishing I could find words for these things in my head. I'd felt like this before, but never this bad. Never this sharp. Like I wanted to peel off my skin. Like I wanted to run away from my life. "Maybe not more, but...different?"

She set down her wine glass and the fact that she was taking me so seriously made me love her with a sharp ache. "Sometimes, yeah."

"What do you want?"

"Sex, mostly," she said with a laugh even though I knew she wasn't joking. "I'd like to be a little more like you—"

I groaned shaking my head. "No, Char. No."

"Stop, Abby, don't do that," she said. "You're always the first to try and knock yourself down. You are so confident in all the ways I'm not, and wanting some of that, wanting to live in my body like that... why isn't that something I should want? You think it's bad just because it's yours."

I held my breath, feeling with sharp clarity how true that was. If I had it, if it was something of mine, something about me—it immediately had less value.

"What do you want?" she asked.

I thought of my savings and that little dream of mine, and I almost told her. But saying the words out loud would make them real. And worse, she would jump on this dream. She'd start building it out of real things. Solid things.

She'd make the dream happen.

And I wasn't ready for that.

I want to change my life, I wanted to say. *I want to be different than this person I've become.*

"California rolls," I said with a sigh. "And a nap."

"Abby, what's wrong?" she asked, not taking the joke.

"Remember Dave?" I said.

Her pale eyebrows lifted over the top edge of her red glasses. "Your shitbag boyfriend from high school?"

I nodded, wishing I hadn't turned down that wine. "Remember how I showed you the black eye and you locked me in our closet and called the cops on Dave?"

"Of course I fucking remember," she said, still flinty and pissed all these years later because Charlotte is, at heart, a badass.

"And I pretended to fight you, remember? I like gave you all this shit, and screamed at you to let me out and for you to butt out of my life."

I'd pounded on the door of our closet, calling her every name in the book, while in my chest my heart was so relieved. My heart had been pudding with gratitude.

"Why are you bringing this up?" she asked. "You're freaking me out."

"Because I went to you so you could do the hard work for me. Make Dave leave me alone. Force my hand into breaking up with him. I went to you because you have always been so strong and I've always been so weak."

"That's not true—"

"Oh my god, Char. We both know that's exactly the truth. You have always saved me. I need to save myself."

She got up and sat next to me on the blue couch. Her arm against mine. Her head against mine. "You've saved me too, Abby," she whispered. "My life would be so small if it weren't for you. I'd be a hermit and I'd be scared all the time, and I would never have a reason to be brave."

We sat there for a while, just next to each other.

"I've met a guy," I said.

"Is that why you're talking about Dave?" she asked, immediately stressed out like I knew she would be. "You've met some asshole and I'm going to have to lock you in the closet again?"

"No." I shook my head for extra emphasis because she didn't believe me, but I'd learned my lesson. "He's not at all like Dave. He's not like any guy I've ever met."

Dave had been small and petty and mean from the minute I met him. Jack was trouble, but he wasn't that kind of trouble. But I needed to be an adult. I needed to take care of myself instead of going, every time, to my sister. Instead of forcing her to take care of me for myself.

"And I think I have to lock myself in the closet," I

said.

"Is he married or something? Why are you saying this?"

"No, he's just… not for me. I want him to be for me. But he's not."

"I'm sorry," my sister sighed after a minute.

"Me too," I sighed right back.

He was a dangerous man. A bad, bad man. And yeah, part of me was perverse and awful, and wanted him more for that reason.

But this was better. Best, even.

Smart.

Which was probably why I didn't like it. Why my whole body wanted to rebel against it. Have a proper tantrum like we were eight again and there was more yellow frosting than pink frosting on the cake—pure proof mom liked Charlotte more than me.

"Sucks being an adult," I said, and Charlotte laughed.

She laughed so hard she snorted, which made me laugh, and in no time we were howling on that loveseat like the kids we'd been.

"Stop," Charlotte cried. "Stop, you're going to make me pee."

"Okay. Stopping." And I held my breath until it sputtered out of me on another laugh.

Finally, we were saved by sushi delivery.

We sat on the rug, our backs against the loveseat, and she told me about the book she was working on and I soaked up every word, so happy that she got to love what she did so much.

And if I was jealous, I ignored it.

If I wanted more, I ignored it.

I'd already adulted enough for one day.

CHAPTER FIVE

Abby

BEFORE

I DECIDED WHEN I got to the bar, I wouldn't ignore Jack, but I wouldn't talk to him either. If we made eye contact, I'd wave. If he stopped to talk, I'd be polite, but not friendly.

I would treat him like a guy I didn't want to have anything to do with the night after I fucked him.

This was a very particular skill I had.

And it was a formidable one, but it felt completely not up to the task of keeping myself away from Jack.

My palms were sweaty as I yanked open the door to the club, but once my eyes adjusted to the dim lighting I realized I shouldn't have worried.

Jack wasn't there. He wasn't reading at the bar. Or standing at the foot of the stairs.

I went into the dressing room to get ready and he wasn't anywhere in that back hallway.

My stomach, despite all my brave words, fell to my

feet with disappointment.

He didn't arrive while the band set up and he didn't come in when the doors opened.

I had a sick feeling that he wasn't here because of me. Because he was avoiding me—or worse, because he got in trouble for last night.

Like Bates fired him?

Guilt twisted hard behind my ribs.

"Where's Jack?" I asked Patty when I could no longer handle not knowing.

"Fuck if I know," Patty said, shaking her head, handing me two cold bottles of vodka to take back to the VIP section. "This place is nuts. Half the time there's twenty guys in suits walking around, the other half there's no one."

I glanced around and didn't see many guys in suits. Just the usual bartenders and servers. A few extra because it was Saturday night.

"Is Bates around?"

She pointed upstairs and then turned around to keep up with the demand at the bar.

Well, one thing I knew for sure, I wasn't going up there. I went back to work and tried to convince myself I didn't care about Jack being there or not.

"Jesus!" Sun shouted over the noise of the crappy

band. We were in the dressing rooms in the second half of the night, regrouping, and she still had to shout over the sound of the band. "This is awful!"

I couldn't argue. Full brass? In this completely cavernous room? Whose idea was that?

There was a real ugly vibe about the place tonight. Like everything was a few wrong moves from blowing up in our faces

And it wasn't just the band. The crowd probably thanks to the band—was shit, too. Dismissive and rude. Demanding.

And worst of all, cheap. We relied on tips and tonight we were seriously coming up short.

"What do we do?" Maria asked. She was shaken, having been back in the VIP section for the last part of the night, and apparently guys back there were getting a little handsy. I was rubbing her back and Sun has handing her tissues and we were all struggling to keep it together.

"Walk the fuck out, I say," Sun said, putting another tissue in Maria's hand.

"Can we do that?" Maria asked.

"I'll talk to someone," I said, because we could leave, but we'd probably lose our jobs. And Maria had a baby at home.

"Who are you going to talk to?" Sun asked. "Scary blonde dude is running up and down those stairs like that shit is on fire. Patty behind the bar is slammed, and your fucking guy is nowhere to be found. I'm telling you, something is happening tonight and we should just get the fuck out."

"I can't lose this job," Maria said. "Not now."

"No one is losing their job," I said. I scowled at Sun, who was pretty great at finding problems, not so great at solving them. "I'll go see if I can't talk to someone upstairs."

That made Sun look at me, her eyes wide.

"What?" I said, even though butterflies had erupted in my stomach. "It's no big deal."

"What do we do while you're upstairs?" Maria asked.

"Work the main room. Stay out of the VIP and stick together," I told them.

Sun saluted me, and feeling a little more confident with her faith in me I headed out of the dressing rooms to see what I could do about salvaging this night.

The bar was stacked about six deep so I didn't even bother trying to talk to Patty. Instead I went right to that staircase.

Tonight there was no one standing there like Jack had been the first night, so there was no one there to stop me.

And a little bit, I wished there was.

Nervous, but more than a little pissed off that there

was no management around to take care of staff, I started up.

It was a fire escape kind of staircase. Narrow and made out of black metal, open all the way up so I could see the bar and dance floor.

Sun and Maria glittered out there in the sea of people.

I was halfway up when the door at the top opened and Bates came out, closing the door behind him.

He didn't see me and for a moment he just stood at the door, his hand squeezing the doorknob so hard his knuckles were white. He really was young. No older than thirty. His bowed head gave the impression of a man in prayer, or a battering ram—like it was all he could do not to bust the door down. Tear it off the hinges.

I turned to run down the stairs, all my courage gone.

But my dress glittered and at my movement he looked up, catching me in the icy clarity of his eyes.

"What are you doing?" he asked over the noise.

"Looking for you!" I cried, angry and scared all at once.

"You found me." He shrugged like the weight on his back was breaking his shoulder.

"We need some help down there!" I gave him the bare bones of what was happening.

"If something doesn't change down there, there's gonna be a fight. Or worse," I finished, proud my voice wasn't cracking.

"Indeed," he said, scanning the crowd, looking weary. If he was any other guy I'd ask him if he even gave a shit. "What needs to happen?"

"You're asking me?"

"You're the only one here."

"Well, you've got to pull the band. This crowd came here to dance, and there's no dancing to this music."

He nodded. "What else?"

"Patty needs about three more people behind that bar."

"There aren't three more people."

"Well, you should find some and fast, otherwise she'll quit. She's swamped back there."

His gaze roved over the first floor and I saw him taking in the truth of what I said. On a roll now, I said, "And you need some muscle to handle the VIP section. It's fucking gross back there. Someone is going to call the cops."

"The cops can not be called." He looked, at that moment, very invested and I hated that I had all these suspicions about why the cops couldn't be called.

"Then you need muscle," I said with a shrug.

"The band and the dancing—can you handle that?"

"Me?"

"Again," he sighed like I was such a trial. "You are the only one here."

"I'm not... I'm not a manager or anything. I'm a shots girl."

"You're being promoted. Can you handle it or not?"

You know what's easy for me? Thinking I can do something. Watching and criticising and mentally redecorating and saving money for a dream I couldn't even say out loud, but never putting myself at risk. Never really doing *anything*.

I was really really good at that.

"Fine," Bates sighed, disappointed in my non-answer. "I'll ask—"

"I can do that," I blurted. "I can."

"I'll get you the muscle." He pulled out his phone and started to text and I still stood there on suddenly shaking legs.

"Is there something else?"

"Jack—"

He looked up fast, his eyes slicing right through me. "What about him?"

"Did you fire him because of what... because of me?"

"He's not fired."

"Is he in trouble?"

"I can understand why he is attracted to you," he said, and the compliment gave me the creeps. "And I can understand his attraction for you. But consider this a friendly warning. He is not like you, and he will drag you down to his hell."

"Drag—"

He bent his head back over his phone, completely dismissing me. I opened my mouth to push for more.

"Leave or you're fired," he said, without looking up, no longer a butler type guy. Totally a gangster type guy.

I turned and scurried down the stairs.

Shelving that entire conversation to the back of my head for dissection later, the first thing I did was head straight across the dance floor to the sound booth.

"Hey," I said to the mixer, who I could tell was trying his best to mitigate the disaster of the horn section.

"Yeah?"

"You need to pull the sound on the band. Put on some dance music."

His eyes narrowed. "No shit," he said. "But I'm not pissing anyone around here off."

"No, Bates told me to do it. This is from them." I pointed up at the second floor.

"Really? In that case." In one swift move he killed the band's mics and pressed play on some track he had cued up on his laptop.

Dance beats flooded the club and the crowd roared, charging the dance floor. The band looked up at the sound booth and gave us the finger.

Sound guy and I winced but high-fived.

Next, I told all the servers to pause on table service and we set up an auxiliary bar on the other side of the club. A giant icy tub of bottled drinks. Bottles of mix and booze for the VIP sections.

The line at the main bar thinned out. Patty shot me a relieved smile.

I was gathering up the nerve to handle the VIP section myself when I felt a buzz in the air. A buzz that was so familiar and so brand new all at the same time.

Please, I thought, closing my eyes for second. And I couldn't say whether I wanted him to be there, or I wanted it to be someone else.

I turned.

And it was Jack behind me. Like my body had known.

This can't be possible.

And yet…it was.

His face, quiet and still, gave no clue to what he was thinking. He was like a deep lake on a cold day. Ominous and compelling all at once.

He wore a trench coat, and rain drops glittered in his dark hair like diamonds.

And he was watching me. Just like I watched him.

I tried to imagine what he saw when he looked at me. The dress, sure; my hair at this point was falling down a little around my face. My lipstick was gone.

I was sweating from setting up the auxiliary bar, and the giant tub had snagged my stockings so there was a hole in the knee.

I was a mess. Like some street urchin in the BBC shows Charlotte forced me to watch.

But I felt like I was glowing. I felt like I was a million feet tall. And I felt like he saw that.

I expected him to head upstairs, but instead he came toward me and my body woke up in a long, slow sizzle. A wave of awareness.

"Hi," he said. Bending toward me so I could hear him over the noise.

"Hi."

There was an awkward pause, the dance music beating like a heart between us.

"Bates brought me in," he said. His breath brushed over my neck and I curled into the sensation.

As a Prince Charming he was a dark knight, but he was my dark knight.

"You're my muscle?"

"I'm your muscle," he said into my ear again. I turned a little toward him, catching his scent, which was odd.

A heavy kind of incense. My parents were Catholic,

and we spent every Sunday at St. Michael's, and he smelled like mass.

I leaned back. "Where did you come from?"

"Does it matter?" he asked. "What do you need me to do?"

Not be this man, I thought. *I need you to just be a guy I met at a bar without the blood and the darkness. And I need you to kiss me, I really really need you to kiss me. Like you did yesterday. I need you to tell me that you don't want me to leave you alone. That you feel this thing between us as much as I do.*

"Abby?"

"VIP," I said quickly.

"What happened?"

"Couple of guys are getting a little grabby with the servers. Maria—"

"Is she all right?"

"Rattled."

"Who touched her?"

Man, I did not want this to be exciting. I tried to resist the caveman charm of a man who would stand up for a woman he didn't know.

"VIP couch two. Guy in the stupid shirt."

"Anyone else?"

"I think if you get rid of him, things will settle down."

"Anyone else gives you a hard time," he said,

"come to me. Sorry I wasn't here earlier."

He lifted a hand as if to touch me. As if to give me a kind of friendly squeeze of the shoulder, and I twitched out of the way. Because I wasn't interested in friendly, and he'd told me to leave him alone. There was no in between for me.

His eyes flared for a moment and he sucked in a quick breath like I'd surprised him.

Hurt him.

Adult, I told myself. *Be a goddamn adult.*

"I'm not scared of you," I told him, imagining what he was thinking. "But…it's better if we don't touch."

His smile was the saddest thing I'd ever seen. And the hook of it sunk deep into me, through my body and into the memories of a sad childhood I did my best to forget. And when he walked away I felt myself tugged along in his wake. The hook in my chest held in his hand.

I told myself I was following to make sure he got the right man, so that he didn't go bull in a china shop and scare people into taking out their phones and uploading video of him beating someone up onto YouTube.

But my worry was superfluous. He was a black sword cutting through the crowds of people, relegating them to inconsequential. Relegating them to nothing. For most of the would-be bad guys, just the sight of him—a real bad guy, his trench coat sweeping behind him like some kind of bad-guy cape—was enough to make them sit up and take notice.

But couch two was a total shit show.

I didn't need to worry that he wouldn't know which guy was the right guy. He walked up to the man in the red and black silk paisley shirt that looked like a costume from *Scarface*.

"Hey!" Jack said like they were old friends.

Scarface had a moment of confusion, and he was holding the knee of the girl next to him so hard her skin was white around his fingers.

"Hey," Jack said into Scarface's blank confusion. "We're waiting for you."

He grabbed Scarface by the shoulder, the other hand grabbing his elbow, and he pulled the guy up off the couch. The woman whose knee he was squeezing sighed with relief. He shuffled the guy down the short hallway between the couches, past me and out into the main club.

"Dressing room door," Jack said as he passed and I hustled ahead to open the door for Jack. It was obvious now that the way he was holding Scarface was causing the guy some pain. And the way he was swearing at Jack would confirm it, but Jack just kept walking, keeping up this kind of hilarious "we're old friends" face. Smiling the whole time.

Honest to God, it looked like Jack was giving the guy the Vulcan Death Grip.

Jack marched him down the hallway, past the bathroom, toward the door that opened out onto the alley. I squeezed ahead of them and opened that door too.

Jack all but pitched the guy out into the rain-slick alley.

"For fuck's sake, man!" the guy yelled, catching his balance against a dumpster and shaking out his arm. "You can't do this!"

"I just did," Jack said.

"What are you? Some piece of shit—" Scarface charged the door, and in one fast move Jack had a gun out and pointed at the guy's face.

A gun.

I jerked backward, tripping on the step and sitting down hard on the ledge of the doorway.

Scarface stopped just inches from the barrel.

"You," Jack said in a quiet voice. "Are not welcome here."

The guy backed up, his hands up, but his face set with anger.

Jack helped me to my feet and then pulled the door shut on the alley. The heavy click of the door shook me loose from the sudden shock the sight of that gun had put me in.

I started backing down the hallway.

"Are you okay?" he asked.

"Fine. All good." I sounded so fake to my own ears, but I couldn't stop. "Thank you."

"Abby," he said in that quiet voice that didn't seem to belong to a man who carried a gun. "I'm sorry if I scared you."

"I'm not scared," I said. But I was lying and we both knew it. "I've got to get back to work."

He nodded like that was what he expected. Like it was his due. "I'm here if you have more problems."

And then he was walking past me out into the bar, leaving behind a trail of incense clinging to the edge of his coat.

THE NEXT FEW hours were gruelling. Managing the crowd was like trying to ride a bull. Not that I'd ever ridden a bull, but it felt like I was white-knuckled through the whole thing.

And the thing I didn't want to think about was how it really wouldn't have been possible without Jack. There was only so much of that club I could control, and he controlled the rest. Coming to my aid without me even having to ask. It was as if he knew what I was worried about and handled it before it became a problem.

All I had to do was think something and he was there, as if I'd radioed him. As if I'd called out. As if he was the only one who could hear me.

I realized at one point that I was dying of thirst and suddenly he was there with a bottle of water.

I didn't know what to do with him. Or how I felt. I didn't know how to keep it to myself, a white-hot coal I was attempting to hold in my bare hands.

When it was finally closing time and Jack helped the last of the stragglers through the door, I nearly collapsed against the bar.

"You killed it tonight," Patty said. "This shit would have gotten ugly without you."

"I could say the same about you."

"Yeah," Patty smiled. "But I wasn't wearing that fucked-up outfit."

I laughed, weary and sore but proud of myself. "I can't wait to take this off."

Sun and Maria had already split, having sold out of the last of the vodka, and I changed by myself in the dressing room. So glad I had leggings, Converse, and an old slouchy sweater to go home in.

I nearly wept when I took off my heels.

I washed my face and took down my hair, only to put it back up in a sloppy bun. The BART station wasn't far and it was a pretty quick ride to my neighborhood, and I'd made this vow to save money for the future and the dream, but the idea of walking there and then waiting…

Tonight deserved an Uber.

But I said that a lot of nights.

I wasn't very good at saving for the dream.

I put my bag over my shoulder, the dress crushed up in a heap in the bottom. Honestly at this point, I couldn't imagine putting it on again. I felt like I'd outgrown it in the span of a few hours.

I pushed open the door and walked through the bar, thanking the cleanup staff, whose job I did not envy, and headed for the door.

"Abby?" Jack stepped out of the shadows.

"Jesus," I said, backing away from him. "You scared me."

"I'm sorry," he said, so formally. Like we hadn't been practically reading each other's mind all night. But the lights were on and room was mostly empty and completely quiet, and everything felt different.

"Do you have a ride?" he asked. "A car?"

"No. I was going to call an Uber."

"I can take you home."

I blinked, that gun a solid real thing. A sharp reality I couldn't ignore.

"That man we kicked out, in the Scarface shirt," he said. "He hasn't left the area. Bates has Sammy taking care of him. But considering everything you've done tonight, let me take you home. On behalf of the club."

"I don't think it's a good idea." I was being an

adult. My sister would be so proud.

"Because of the gun?"

He said it. Just like that. Naming what I'd been too scared to name.

"Because of a lot of things. But yeah… the… gun doesn't help."

He leaned forward as if to tell me a secret. We were in the coat check area, a small foyer, so there was no place for me to go.

It was me and him and the dark and everything I knew I shouldn't want, but did anyway.

"The gun is empty," he whispered.

"Empty?"

"Shhhh." He pulled me by the elbow away from the door, further into the shadows. "I don't need everyone knowing that."

"That you carry around an unloaded gun?"

"Yes."

"Is it always unloaded?"

He sighed. "Yes."

That made zero sense.

"So…you're just pretending to be a bad guy?"

The white of his teeth gleamed. "I'm a bad guy. And nine times out of ten an unloaded gun does the exact same job as a loaded one."

"Which is?"

"Scare people."

I blinked, imagining that was true. It certainly worked on Scarface shirt guy. And me. It really worked on me.

But what happens the tenth time?

"Let me take you home," he said. "All Uber does is increase credit card debt."

I laughed at him.

"Credit card debt? That's what you're worried about?"

"No. I'm worried about how exhausted you are and how I'd like to take care of you. Just a little."

He'd read my mind all night, and now he cared. The webs of connection between us were thick and impossible to ignore.

"You can sit in the back seat," he said. "Have me drop you off at the corner so I don't know where you live."

It was like he not only knew the parameters of the cage I would build for him, but he was actually helping me build it so I could feel safe.

That, more than the confession about the gun, convinced me.

"Okay," I said. "I would love a ride."

He nodded, his face so carefully still. But somehow I knew I'd made him happy. It was like his chemistry changed, some internal light that only I could see binged on.

CHAPTER SIX

Abby

BEFORE

WE WENT OUT the side door into the chill of San Francisco. We were South of Market, a little further south than the really hip places. It was seedier here, the smell of salt water thick in the air.

He hit the button on his key fob and the lights on a black sedan across the street blinked on and off. He opened up the back seat for me and I rolled my eyes.

"I don't think that's totally necessary," I said, and he shut the door with a nod and a small smile. It was like my attraction was a banked fire and the fear that had doused it was gone, and I could feel the heat coming back.

My promises to try and be an adult felt like empty threats against the power of this feeling.

The inside of the car smelled even more like church.

"Why does your car smell like Mass?" I asked after

he sat down in the driver seat and started the car.

He put the car in drive. "I was at church when Bates called me for help."

"Church?" I asked. "Really?"

"Church. Really. Where am I taking you?"

I gave him the address for my place, a good twenty-minute drive away.

"So…what exactly are you?" I asked.

He glanced over, his eyebrow raised. "What am I?"

"You carry a gun. But it's not loaded. You work for Lazarus, who is—"

"Nothing you should say out loud or to anyone. Ever."

His scowl meant business, but I was too tired and too high from my night to be entirely cowed.

"You read books in bars."

"You listen to them at the gym."

He said that like there was no difference between us.

"But we're talking about you. Yesterday you were covered in blood and today you go to church. I can't keep up with all these pieces of you."

"I'm a man, Abby. Just a man."

The way he said it put a lance through my stomach, pinning me to the seat, making it hard to breathe. It was a warning in a way, a declaration.

I am a man.

My hormones turned over like some dumb dog looking for a belly scratch. The attraction was back and better than ever. It was attraction with a vengeance.

This ride home might not have been the best idea if my intention was to stay away from him.

And then as if to make everything worse, in the silence of the car, my stomach absolutely roared. Like in three-part harmony, for at least five seconds.

My stomach growled so loud that Jack looked at me, shocked.

"Are you all right?" he asked. "Is there… a dog in your backpack?"

"No. It's my stomach."

"That wasn't a dog?"

"No, I just haven't eaten—"

"Ever?"

"Okay, let's not get carried away."

"Would you like some breakfast?" he asked. "Or dinner. I guess." He glanced at this watch. "It's two a.m. You could pick."

Weighing the pros and cons, gauging my bravery and possibly my stupidity, took a long time. So long that the light faded from his face and it was sad to see it go. It felt rare and it felt precious and I wanted more of it.

"I would love breakfast," I said. "There's a Denny's not too far."

He gave me a little scowl, even though he seemed to be glowing just for me. "We can do better than that."

"Well, lead on, breakfast man."

Instead of turning right to merge onto the highway, he pulled a U-turn in the deserted road and headed south. His sleek sedan made short work of the twisty roads leading us along the back way toward South San Francisco. A fairly shitty town near the airport.

"Really?"

"Trust me," he said. "Best diner in the Bay area."

"Do they have pie?" I asked. "Because if we're coming all the way out here, I'm going to need pie."

"They have pie. Homemade pie, even."

His grin was cocky and I realized the farther we got away from the Moonlight Lounge, the easier he seemed. And I wondered briefly what would happen if we kept on driving, through the last of the night, into the dawn.

Would he take off that tie? Roll up his sleeves? Would he smile more? Laugh? I imagined us on Highway 1, the sun coming up over the mountains, his hand on the back of my seat.

I imagined him a different person.

I imagined myself a different person.

"Abby?" he asked in the manner of a guy who'd been trying to get my attention for a few moments.

"Sorry," I said. The vision of us in the sunrise so

clear it was disarming. "Got caught in a daydream."

"About what?"

"I was wondering what would happen if we just kept driving." I was bold with guys, but this was out there even for me. Perhaps it was the exhaustion making me so reckless, making me reveal so much.

He glanced at me, his face blank with a kind of astonishment.

"I can't," he whispered.

"I can't either. That's why it's a daydream."

"Where would you go?" he asked. "If you could keep driving?"

"Idaho," I said without skipping a beat.

He blinked at me, laughing.

"It's a long story," I said. "But I would go to Idaho. What about you?"

"I don't know."

"Come on, you must have someplace you'd escape to."

"I don't."

"Jack—"

"There's no escape," he said, not snapping at me but ending the conversation.

I was about to apologize—for what, I had no idea—but he cleared his throat and said, "It was a good thing you were there tonight."

"I don't know. Someone would have figured things

out," I said with fumbling modesty.

No escape. From what? What does he mean?

He laughed. "Maybe in a regular club."

The Moonlight Lounge was far from regular.

"Is it a front?" I asked, not entirely sure of the lingo.

"It's a vanity project. The Moonlight is just a thing Lazarus thinks he should have."

A thing he thinks he should have. The words resonated through me, making me silent. Making me think. I'd spent a lot of time thinking that about things I wanted. Like wanting something was the only justification I needed for having it.

"Tell me something," he said. "Why are you wasting time giving away shots when you could be managing clubs?"

"It's a job," I said, immediately defensive because my sister asked me this all the time. "And a pretty high-paying one. It's not wasting time."

"I'm sorry," he said, taking his eyes off the road to watch me. "You just seemed so on fire tonight. So in your element."

"Tonight was the only time I've ever done anything like that."

"Really?"

It was a heady thing to have Jack see me as so capable. And to have him listen to me without question. It was like a drug, almost. And I was high on it.

"Really."

"But you knew exactly what to do."

"It's not that hard," I said, chipping at the polish on my thumb. It was already ruined. I'd have to redo it before our next gig. "Work in enough bars and I think it's probably pretty obvious to anyone who pays attention."

He made a low sound in his throat, driving with one hand draped across the top of the steering wheel. "That's the thing, isn't it? Most people don't pay attention."

"It wouldn't have gone so well without you there," I said.

His grin was wry. "I'll be your backup any day."

He slowed to a stop in front of a lit-up bank of windows in an otherwise dark stretch of buildings.

The J in the Jim's Diner neon sign was burned out, the apostrophe was flickering, gasping its last breaths. Inside, weary waitresses in white button-down shirts took orders from truckers, washed in golden light from the lamps over the tables.

"It doesn't look like much," he said. "But it's good."

It looked simple and basic. Nothing fake.

It looked like an oasis. An island in a dark sea.

"It's perfect," I said.

We got out of the car and it was warmer here, away

from the water. Jack waited for me on the curb, his eyes focused on an old apartment building across the street. The sign, Shady Oaks, sculpted in wrought iron arching across the entryway.

He stood there a long time, the wind whistling down the street.

"You know that place?" I asked, standing beside him as we looked at the dark apartment building. It looked like a relic of some kind, the architecture, the empty pool in the courtyard. Like something left behind. For people who had been left behind.

"Not really," he said.

I wanted to ask then why we were staring at it. But he turned, his hand grazing the small of my back as he turned us toward the diner. "Let's feed you before your stomach eats you from the inside."

The bell rang over our heads as we walked in, and the smell of potatoes and coffee and bacon made my stomach growl again. Jack, beside me, smiled and lifted two fingers up for the hostess.

"Away from the window," he said and she nodded, grabbing two menus for us.

Jack ordered coffee and I had a water and a hot tea.

"So," I asked, shrugging out of my coat, watching the way he tried not to watch me. It was warm in this back booth. Cozy. The sound of the kitchen and the conversation in the other booths were insulation. It felt like the world was far away. "How do you know this place?"

"My mom was a diner expert." He smiled as he said it. Flipping his spoon over as he talked, watching his own fingers because it was easier than watching me.

I understood the impulse.

"This was a favorite?" I asked.

"One of many. There was not a diner in the entire Bay area we didn't spend some Sunday afternoon in. We'd go to church, confession, and then it was diner time."

"What did she like about diners?"

"All of it. People bringing her food. The endless cups of coffee. My brother was picky as hell but he would always eat pancakes, so it was a meal without a fight." He shrugged. "And what's not to like about a diner?"

"Nothing," I said with a smile. "Does she still go to diners?"

"She died, years ago."

"I'm sorry."

"Me too," he said. "She left a big hole when she was gone that we all tried to fill."

"You have a brother?"

"Yeah, a younger brother. I mean, I do in a technical sense, but we aren't really... talking, these days."

"Oh no." I was really bringing the bummer tonight.

"I haven't actually seen him in two years."

"Oh my god, I couldn't even imagine not seeing my sister for two days, much less two years."

The waitress arrived with my little tin pot of hot water and I got busy unwrapping my tea bag and getting everything just right.

"Your sister, is she older or younger?" he asked.

"We're twins."

"Jesus," he said. "There are two of you walking around?"

"We're not identical."

"Probably a good thing. The men of San Francisco could not take two of you."

"We're really different, actually. She's like an artist. Lives in her head most of the time. Kind of hates people. Or is scared of them. Hard to say."

"That's my brother. Only not an artist. He's an athlete. But he definitely hates people."

"We should introduce them."

"So she could be scared of him?"

"She's tougher than she thinks. She'd survive."

He smiled at me so wide he revealed a chipped tooth. One of the incisors. But then, as if he realized what he'd revealed, he lifted his hand to rub his mouth, hiding the flaw. And I wanted to tell him not to bother. That there was no need to be embarrassed. Or hide. I liked the flaws.

I took a sip of my tea, burning my tongue because it was still too hot, but I could not say these things. I didn't know how much further down the rabbit hole I could go with this man and survive the trip.

"What sport does your brother play?" It was so much easier to ask him about his brother instead of him. And it was obvious that he was so much happier talking about his brother instead of talking about himself.

His face was relaxed, his wavy dark hair falling into his eyes, and my fingers twitched as I imagined how his hair would feel against my skin.

I imagined doing it, just reaching forward and sweeping it away from his eyes. I imagined how still he would get with surprise, how startling it would be for both of us.

But how it would be a relief too.

I imagined him closing his eyes, the relief of my touch would be so sharp. So clear. Too much almost in this restraint we had between us. This carefully choreographed not touching we were doing.

"He's a wrestler," Jack was saying, and I snapped back into the conversation, embarrassed by my daydreams. "Now he does some kind of MMA thing. He's good at it. Like scary good."

"Is it dangerous? The MMA thing."

"Of course. He wouldn't do it if it wasn't." He took

a sip of his coffee and then frowned when he realized the cup was empty. "Where are your parents?" he asked. "Still in the city?"

"Florida," I said. "They used to just go part of the time, but a few years ago they sold their house up here and stayed there year round."

"You miss them?"

"Not as much as you would think. My parents didn't really parent us. They kind of left my sister and me alone to raise each other. I was sick as a kid."

"Sick? With what?"

"Allergies. Asthma. I missed most of second grade because I was in and out of the hospital with pneumonia. And then my sister missed most of second grade because she wouldn't go to school if I wasn't going. And I think Mom tried to kind of split us up and find a way to be in between us so she could be in our lives, but we were just such a unit. Such a team, we didn't let anyone in. We still haven't," I said with a laugh.

"What do you mean?"

It was strange how far this conversation had gotten, like we'd just been drifting down this river and I was only now looking up to see how unfamiliar this territory was.

"Neither one of us has had serious boyfriends. Or real friends either. It's still us against the world." I wrinkled my nose at him. "That is weird, isn't it?"

"I don't know," he said with a shrug. "It seems kind of nice. I tried so hard to be on a team with my brother that I joined the high school wrestling team, just so we could do it together."

"High school wrestling?" I asked, smiling.

"Desperate times," he said with a smile. "I would have joined the marching band for my brother, and I have no musical ability at all."

"Hold on," I said, closing my eyes. "I'm just trying to imagine you…"

It was a fucking delight to imagine this dangerous man as a kid. An awkward high school student. A gangly wrestler. Curly hair sprouting up from his head gear.

"It wasn't pretty," he said. And I couldn't agree, but I said nothing.

"Were you any good?"

"I was terrible."

"You're joking."

"Awful. Like the worst kid on the team."

"And you did it anyway?"

"For Jesse? Yeah. Practice and the meets, the bus rides to the meets, that was seriously the best time we spent together. What was a little public humiliation?"

The laughter dried up from his face, his blue eyes lost their bright lights, and I imagined that both of us were wondering how those two boys in the back of a high school bus could grow up to not speak to each other.

I couldn't connect those two dots. Something dark happened in between them, the brothers and the dots making their connection drop.

"You sound like a good brother," I said.

"No. I've made a lot of mistakes." He shook his head, the spoon for once still against the table. "But you sound like a good sister," he said.

"It's my sister who was good."

"I don't believe you," he said with serious earnest eyes.

"I'm trying," I said, "to be different than I was. To be better. I let a lot of shit happen because she felt guilty and I felt mad, and the whole world expected less of me and more of her, and I just took advantage of that for so long." I shook my head, my face suddenly hot. Why did I keep talking like this? "That doesn't make any sense," I said.

"It makes perfect sense," he said. "My brother and I had a similar situation. I just… took care of things, you know. Like that was my job. Trying to clear the path for him."

"That's what my sister did for me."

"She sounds special," he said.

"I should introduce her to you. She's so smart. She reads all the time too, you know."

He narrowed his eyes at me. "Are you trying to fix me up with your sister?"

I laughed. "You'd probably like her better."

"Impossible," he said, whispered really into the still warm air between us, like a ship setting sail from his side of the booth making its way over to mine.

Our gazes held, awkward and naked. So much revealed.

He coughed, looked away, and I sagged slightly in the booth, feeling panicked nearly at my vulnerability with this man. How I'd been caught out. It didn't sit well with me, this vulnerability—it made my hard edges want to come out.

He looked out the window, at the dark city outside. He was younger, right now, than he usually seemed. His dark hair flopping over his forehead, his shirt sleeves rolled up revealing his arms and tattoos. His blue eyes sad.

"Do you always get what you want?" he asked.

I took a sip of my tea and tilted my head, like I was pondering the weight of his question. "What do you think?"

"I think you get what you want."

"I think you're right."

And I want you.

I didn't say the words, but they were there just the same like a tiny skywriter had just written them in the air between us.

"What about you?" I asked. "Do you get what you want?"

"Never," he said.

I blinked. "You never get what you want?"

"I never reach for what I want. I never acknowledge what I want. The second I want something I do everything in my power to forget it exists."

"You tried to do that to me," I whispered.

"And now look at us."

"So… what does that make me?"

"Trouble."

"I've heard that before."

"And special."

Like the words set a match to a fire I hadn't noticed, or couldn't see, the atmosphere around us completely changed. The smile faded from his face and those blue eyes were hot and intense and I couldn't breathe.

Desire, a dark and sudden lust, turned my bones to butter and I could only sit there and feel the power of him.

What have I done? I wondered in some distant way. *This is too much. He is too much.*

It was easy to toy with boys, young men with money in their pocket who liked the idea of a woman who looked like me on their arm.

But Jack... he was looking at me like he wanted to consume me. I like was something he *needed*. He told me himself he was a man. And I'd had so few men in my life. Boys sure. Guys.

Not men.

And none of them like him.

I looked back down at my tea, adding more milk. Spilling sugar everywhere.

"I can call you a cab," he said. His voice low, slightly embarrassed like he'd revealed too much and he knew it. "We don't have to eat."

In about a month from this moment, I'd think about this and how so many things combined to keep me there. To put me and Jack on the road to disaster and pain.

I should have grabbed my coat and gone. Never looked back.

But I wasn't very smart. Reckless was my middle name.

And the waitress arrived and asked, "What can I get you?"

And my body answered: *Jack.*

"Abby?" he asked. "You don't have to stay."

"I'll have the pancakes," I said, handing the menu over to the waitress.

Jack smiled, just a little twist to his lips and he was so handsome, so fully himself and fully a man, that my heart literally skipped a beat.

He ordered eggs over easy, and the moment to avoid our own end was over.

"What's next for you after the Moonlight?" he asked.

"Wherever they send me," I said with a shrug.

"You saving for school or something? College?"

"I'm just a shots girl," I said, keeping mum on the subject of my little nest egg and the dream.

"That's hardly true."

"But it is."

"You could run that club," he said.

"Someone needs to. You telling me I should try for the job?"

"I'm saying you could do it. In a heartbeat. But you shouldn't work there."

"You shouldn't work there either," I said.

"Ten minutes in my car and you think you know?" he asked.

"One glance of you reading at that bar and I knew," I said. "Why aren't you going to college?" he asked.

"You're changing the subject."

"I am. Why aren't you going to college?"

"Lots of reasons."

"You're not interested?"

"No, but I'm not very smart," I said, wondering why in the world I was telling him this.

"That's bullshit."

"No, it's pretty much public record. Years of report cards don't lie. My sister, she got all the brains."

"School only measures one kind of smart."

"Well, it's the only kind that matters in this world."

"My brother was terrible at school," he said, arranging his knife and fork in a particular way. "But that doesn't make him not smart."

"You don't know me, Jack."

"I know you're smart about the club. About people. I know you're a natural manager and those girls you work with look to you as a leader. That makes you pretty smart."

I could feel myself blushing. Like a bad one, like from school when I'd get called up to the board to answer some simple math problem, only the numbers would be inside out and I'd be so scared I couldn't do anything.

"Thank you," I murmured. "That's… no one's said that to me before."

"That can't be true."

I flipped back my hair and gave him a level look. "What do you think men say to me?"

His eyes took me in in pieces. My long white-blonde hair. My sparkling blue eyes. My cheekbones and collarbones, sharp enough to cut glass.

"I can imagine."

"Right. Not a whole lot of compliments on my brain."

"Then they aren't seeing you the way I see you."

They weren't empty, these compliments. They were real because nothing about this man pandered or lied. It was obvious. It was why I was attracted to him.

"What about you?" I asked. "You're so smart, reading on the job and everything. You go to college?"

"I dropped out after three years."

"Dropped out?"

"Two years ago."

"Why?"

"Family stuff."

"Your mom?"

"No, she died when we were in high school."

My heart stuttered for him, squeezed in my chest in recognition of the difficulty of his choices. "You should go back. You must have been close to getting a degree."

"I'm about ten credits short of a degree in economics."

My jaw fell open, which made him laugh. "Get the fuck out. Economics?"

He nodded, looking slightly embarrassed and also pleased at the same time.

"What were you going to do with that degree?" I asked. I'm not sure I'd ever met anyone with a degree in economics.

"No idea," he said. "Grad school, probably. Law school maybe."

"Jesus."

"It was so long ago, I'm not even sure who I was at that time."

"It was two years ago!" I cried.

"Right." He shook his head like he couldn't believe it either. "But so much happened. I feel like that kid I'd been, he was someone I knew a long time ago. Someone from the neighborhood or something. An acquaintance."

"I'm sorry," I said, reaching out across this table, because I could see that these old wounds still hurt. The blood was fresh. I touched his hand and fast as a snake, he grabbed me. My fingers in his. It wasn't hard, his hold on me. But it was firm. And hot and real and I curled my fingers around his, like his hand was the only thing keeping me from blowing out the window.

He looked at me, a long time, long enough that I felt naked and not in a good way. Not in the way I liked or was used to. For the first time in a very long time, I felt awkward.

"I don't know what you want from me," I breathed.

He didn't let go of my hand and we both sat there like the rest of the world didn't exist, and he'd been sending me so many mixed messages I didn't know what to do. I felt brand new to this game.

"Everything," he said, his voice a low gruff whisper, full of intention and heat.

Our eyes caught, tangled and I couldn't look away. I couldn't breathe or think. And for a second I was sure I was going to crawl across the table into his lap.

Or maybe he was going to shove the table out of the way, get down on his knees in front of me, and hold my face in his hands.

And he would kiss me. And it wouldn't be like any other kiss I'd ever had. It would change everything. It would change me.

It was so powerful, this kiss, I could taste it. I could feel it unraveling me.

And it hadn't even happened.

"So?" I said in a voice that just barely didn't shake. "What are you going to do about it?"

He pulled out his wallet, threw down forty dollars and stood up.

"Let's go," he said.

CHAPTER SEVEN

Abby

BEFORE

I WAS TUGGED along behind him like a small ship bouncing around in the wake of a bigger ship.

It's not like I looked to give up my power or my will, but I was pretty happy when the chance came to hand it over to him and I gave it up willingly.

Breathlessly.

Tired of fighting this thing between us.

At the car he pushed me against the passenger side door, my body between him and the cold metal of the sedan.

"Are you sure?" he asked. "You have to be sure. I can't—"

Instead of answering, I kissed him. And it wasn't his careful kiss from the other night. This was my kiss. Full of *my* hunger. Full of *my* desire.

Fiercer than I'd ever been. Than I'd ever felt.

I pulled him to me by his jacket and I all but forced

my way into his mouth. He tasted like mint and heat and coffee, and he quickly became my favorite flavor.

"Get in the car," he said, pulling away. He opened the door behind my butt and all but pushed me inside. He ran around to the driver side and was in the car and driving between one deep breath and the next.

He turned left at the corner and then right, back toward the city.

"I'm at—"

"We're going to my place," he said.

Fine. That was fine. I mean, was it dangerous… maybe. Did I care? Fuck no.

I kept my hands to myself, curled them into my lap, pressed my legs together, trying to shrink almost into my skin so I didn't reach out for him.

I couldn't even look at him.

I had to contain this feeling. But it was hard. So hard. When all I wanted to do was touch him.

"Are we close?" My voice shook.

He groaned low and deep in his throat. "Five more minutes, princess."

I nodded stiffly and glanced out the window. Jumping when I felt his hand against my leg. I closed my eyes, focused on breathing as his hand crept higher up my thigh.

"Look at me," he said and my head rolled across the seat back so I could focus on him. God, he was handsome. And he was not scowling or blank-faced. He was focused and he looked, when he glanced my way, like he wanted to eat me up.

I shifted in my seat, spreading my legs, giving him room to play if that was what he wanted.

He smiled, his eyes back on the road but his hand finding its way beneath the sweater to cup me, the hot damp core of me in his palm. Separated only by my thin leggings.

"You're wet," he breathed like he was rather astonished by that.

"I am."

"Hot."

I nodded, gulping down air.

"Does it hurt, princess?" he asked. His fingers squeezing me, just a little. Just enough. I moaned. "Does it hurt wanting so much?"

"It does," I breathed.

He turned two left turns, and he stopped, put the car in park. In the silence without the engine, all I could hear was my breathing. My heart beating. We were in the parking area behind some condos, surrounded by dumpsters and other cars. One streetlight turned the air to gold around us, and when he looked at me, his face was dark. Completely shadowed.

"I want to make you come," he said.

I knew what he meant. He meant right here. In this golden air, the chill of the night on the other side of the car. If we got out, the chill might get to us. We'd have to navigate doors and locks. Walk down hallways. There would be all this time and space for this feeling, this nuclear-level threat of combustion to leach away.

I didn't want that either.

"Please," I whimpered.

He unclipped my seat belt and pulled my hips lower in the seat. I felt like a puddle against the leather. This seemed fast. We'd kissed twice. And now his hand was slipping down the front of my leggings. It should seem weird. Weirder. But it felt so perfectly right. Like an antidote.

My entire body was tense. So tense when his fingers brushed the top of my underwear I jumped. His eyes, suddenly wary, flew to mine and his fingers, the rough scrape of them over sensitive skin, stopped.

"It's okay," I whispered with a shaky laugh. "It's good."

"We don't—"

"Please," I said, wondering why we sounded like two virgins on prom night. Wondering why I felt like a virgin on prom night (not that I had been a virgin on my prom night, but still). I put my hand over his, pressing it down between my legs, his finger pushing through the damp seam of my pussy, brushing over my clit.

Making both of us gasp.

I couldn't look into his eyes anymore; it was far too much intimacy with a man whose last name I didn't even know.

Don't. Don't think of that stuff.

Who needed last names when we had this fucking connection?

I could feel him shifting next to me, finding an easier angle down my pants, and I wanted to smile, laugh even at us, because there was a part of this that was ridiculous.

But then he scraped the slick side of his fingernail against my clit. Pressed it down like a hard shell against me and I opened my eyes, blinking at the new sensation. He pushed harder, slid the fingernail against me, finding the edge and using that against me too until I couldn't keep silent.

My moan was a garbled *what* and *more* combined, and he seemed to understand my stupid language because he gave me more. His lips found my neck and my head fell sideways, my legs spread wider, and he rolled my clit under his finger like it was a pebble. The bottom of my foot began to burn, some random nerve going berserk, and his tongue traced the curve of my ear, and somehow it was all enough.

It was barely anything really. His tongue and the

touch of his finger, but I felt myself about to come. The great wave of a rogue orgasm spreading out through my body and then—

He stopped.

"What?" I breathed, my eyes open to find him a few inches from me. So intent. So dark and wild. "Why did you stop?"

"You're so beautiful," he said. "Just like this. Just on the edge." He touched me again, his finger against my clit as if to hold me there.

"Please," I breathed. This game was not unfamiliar, but I'd never been so willing a player in it. I'd said these words before but now, in this increasingly cold car, with this sometimes cold man, I meant them down to my blood vessels.

"And now," he said, with a slice of a smile. "You beg me. How did I get this lucky?"

I would fall to my knees in front of this man. I—in fact—could not wait to do it.

"Please," I moaned. "It hurts."

He flinched. "I'm sorry." And then his finger pressed against me like he knew my favorite touch, or perhaps—this, him now, was my new favorite touch. Everything was rewired inside of me. Everything was different. New.

"Yes," I sighed as the wave came back, bigger and higher than before. My hands jerked out as if to keep me in place, as if the wave were a real thing, threatening to take me up and out of this car, away from him.

The cold of the glass barely registered against my palm, but I felt the rough scrape of his beard against my other hand.

"I want to be inside you," he said.

"Yes. Yes. Inside."

Did he want to fuck in this car? We could do that. I could just—

But then his fingers speared into me, thick and hard and I jerked, crying out. It was unexpected but right. So right. The rightest thing I'd ever felt. He was whispering things into my ear, soft words I couldn't understand. I couldn't hear him through the roar of my blood.

My hips jerked and the waves crashed and I held onto the collar of his coat so hard my fingers cramped.

"Fuck!" I cried and cried again. My hips rocking against his fingers.

I was blind and dumb to anything but this pleasure.

And then suddenly it was over, and just as suddenly he was gone. Out of the car, cold air blasting over me, and then the door shut. With fumbling fingers, I tried to fix my pants, my brain still buzzing.

What was—

And then my door was open and he was there, lifting me up and out of his car. He didn't put me on my feet. No, like the Prince Charming I'd said he wasn't, he swept me up into his arms.

"My bag," I said.

And he ducked down enough so I could grab it. And then he shut the door with his hip and walked us in through what looked like the back door of a condo unit.

Small details registered and then vanished. So much security. Fences with touchpad locks. He lowered my feet at the door, his arm still around my waist, holding me so tight against him I could feel his erection through our clothes. I leaned up to kiss him, the hard line of his mouth irresistible in this mix of back yard shadow and light.

"Stop," he said, putting his key in the lock. "Give me a second."

Rebuffed, I leaned back and he glanced at me. "Kiss me now and I will fuck you against this door, and I don't want to do that."

"I don't want to do that either." But a little bit, I did.

"Then…" He blew out a breath and pulled in another one like he was trying to calm his hands. "Let me just—" He made a noise as the key slipped into the lock and then turned. There were two more locks like that, and finally he pulled me into the condo behind him, and it was dark but quiet and I heard his keys hit something hard, the floor maybe, but then it stopped mattering because his arms were back around me and he was kissing me.

No more absolution. No more forgiveness. This was a kiss with need and hunger and pain in it. It was too much almost, like hearing something so honest it hurt. It was a kiss that rocked me backward and I would have stepped back, but for his arm around my back, pulling off my jacket.

And then I was pulling off his jacket. And I was kissing him in the same way, like I was transferring the weight and pain of all my secrets and all my doubts onto him, and he took them without question.

Oh my god, I thought, dimly in the very back of my head, the only place I could still think in words. *This man will ruin me.*

His jacket hit the ground, and I didn't stop to bother with his shirt. I pulled at his belt, the zipper of his pants until I had the hard warm length of his cock in my hand.

He jerked, flinched almost like it was too much, just my fingertips against his skin, so I put my hand around him, holding his cock in my fist. My thumb slipping over the top, where he was wet.

And here's the thing about me: I don't give blow jobs. I don't like them. I don't like the mess of them, the fuss, the uncomfortable intimacy of my mouth around a man's dick. I don't like the power dynamic.

I don't like them and I don't give them.

But I went down to my knees in front of Jack because I wanted to. Because that was all I wanted. And I licked him, from bottom to top and tasted him. *Tasted Jack.*

And the intimacy I'd flinched away from all my sexual life was suddenly exactly right.

Rough, his fingers speared into my hair, pulling it as he cupped my head, cradling it in his hands as he pushed into my mouth. The tip of his cock brushing the back of my throat.

I shouldn't like this.

I shouldn't want it.

But I did.

"Yes, princess," he breathed as he fucked into my mouth. "Take it. Just like that."

I did, over and over, spit running down my chin, my eyes closed, an inferno blazing under my skin. Until finally he stopped me. I moaned in protest, but he pulled me up onto my feet.

For a second I got a glimpse of his eyes, wild and fierce, and I wondered if I should feel afraid, but I couldn't even muster up the thought.

He turned me, until my back was against his front and his hands at my waist. He didn't just shove my leggings down—he tore them.

He tore them off my body and I screamed at the sound, so turned on by the violence, so close to coming I couldn't believe it. I didn't feel like me and I'd never felt better.

His hand cupped me again, his fingers slipping between the very wet lips of my pussy.

"Come with me," he said, walking forward, and I laughed because I didn't have a choice. I didn't have a choice even if he wasn't holding me practically off my feet, against his chest.

We walked through a dark kitchen and a dark living room and into a bedroom.

Frosty white light came in through a high window, revealing the snowy landscape of his bed, surrounded by shelves and shelves of books. Books were stacked on the ground in the shadows by the bed. We stepped forward and I knocked over one of the stacks.

"Sorry," I breathed, bending over as if to clean it up, and the press of my ass against his dick made him groan. Made him fold over my body, his lips at my shoulder.

"I'm going to fuck you," he said. "I can't wait. I can't stop."

Instead of picking up the books I put my hands against the end of the bed and pushed harder against him, not sure how much more permission I could give him.

But apparently that was enough. There was fumbling behind me and I looked over my shoulder to see him tearing open the silver packet of a condom. Again I had that sensation of the two of us being kids doing this for the first time—that's the lack of finesse he had with that condom.

But then his hand was on my hip and his cock was at the entrance to my body

"Are you ready?" he asked.

"So ready."

With a plunge he was inside me and I swallowed back a scream of surprise and pleasure. He was hard and heavy and thick and long and perfect. And I felt him everywhere, the tips of my fingers and the bottom of my feet.

I tore off my sweater, flinging it into the unknown, and he groaned his approval at the sight of my back, of my skin. His hands, spread wide over my shoulders as he pushed harder into me. Eased back and pushed harder. A steady rhythm that made my toes curl and my eyes close. That made my body clench and shiver like it was thing without control.

And I was. He was. He pushed forward again and my arms gave out and I sprawled against the bed and he followed me down, lifting my hips to keep taking him. Steady and steady and steady. He was the earth turning. The tides in the sea. The sun and moon in a constant cycle.

I put my finger between my legs, finding my clit in the slick of heat and come between my legs, because I had to come or I had to stop.

And I didn't want to stop.

"Yes," he said. "Yes. Make yourself come."

I needed no other encouragement. No other sensation but him inside of me and my finger against my clit. There was no wave this time, only a lightning strike. Every muscle in my body curled and every blood vessel contracted and I saw stars and I screamed and I lost myself for just a moment in the white-hot blaze of my orgasm.

And still he was steady. He never stopped. A metronome of fucking. Inexhaustible.

"Please," I said.

"More?"

"No. No. You come."

He stopped. And I felt his stillness behind me. I shifted my hips, feeling him hard inside my body. Fucking him in half measures because of our angles and my body's exhaustion.

"Jack," I breathed, turning my head. "Please. I want you to come."

I didn't know why he stopped. And I didn't know why he started again, but his hands fell onto the bed beside me and he pummeled me. I could only lie there, boneless and replete, a soft place for every wild thrust to land.

It didn't hurt. Or if it did, it wasn't the kind of hurt I felt at that moment. I turned my head, craning my neck so I could see his face.

See the very careful reader's face as he came undone.

IIIs head tipped back and he roared. His face red and sweating. His eyes closed. He jerked into me, a thing without power or control. A wild shudder rippled through him and then… it was over.

He fell down beside me on the bed, careful with the condom, careful with my body. He stared up at the ceiling. Again unreadable.

But it didn't stop me from trying. From watching him and gathering clues in the bright flush on his cheeks, the sweat tricking down his face from his hairline. But he didn't turn. And he didn't say anything.

The longer I lay there, the colder I got. The facts as I knew them crept in through the bubble of lust we'd created.

I know next to nothing about this guy, and what I do know is bad. Dangerous.

As much as some romantic, foolish part of me might want that to be different, or might believe that his job wasn't all he was—the facts remained.

Bad man. He said it himself.

I urged myself to get up, to find my sweater, to leave and not look back, but my body was in no mood to obey.

Get up! I told myself, and like I'd said it out loud he turned to face me, just his head. His eyes slumberous and quiet. His entire body still and replete.

The urge to touch him was impossible to resist, and my fingers found his hair and pushed it back from his forehead, the way I'd wanted to the minute I met him.

"I will take you home, if that's what you want," he said, his voice a rough whisper. "I'll call you a cab. I'll leave and you can stay here alone. Whatever you want. And I don't say this to change your mind or influence you in any way, I say it only because I want to, but I would like you to stay. With me. If you'd like to."

He was blushing again and I was so charmed. So physically awash, so quiet inside my own body that the idea of leaving was preposterous.

This man who didn't ask for what he wanted, was asking me to stay.

"It's safe here. I promise," he said, as if trying to convince me. But I needed no convincing.

"I'll stay," I said. "With you."

And his smile was a sunrise.

"Do you want some food?" he asked. "I haven't fed you—"

"Sleep," I said, my eyelids dipping. So many orgasms, I could barely stay awake. "Let's just sleep. You can feed me later."

He nodded and stood up beside the bed, where he shed his clothes like a skin. The fine shirt and the shoes he hadn't bothered to take off. The pants, the belt clanking against the floor as they landed. He grabbed the top of the fluffy white quilt. The sheets beneath it were pale gray, and I shifted and he lifted me and helped me, and then I was in his bed with him beside me.

We faced each other and it felt like there was a lot I should say, but I didn't know the words again. My limited vocabulary could not put its arms around this feeling.

"Thank you," I whispered, touching his face again because it was so handsome and so close.

He laughed, a warm gust of air over my hand.

"Go to sleep," he said.

And I did, feeling impossibly safe in this dangerous man's bed.

CHAPTER EIGHT

Abby

BEFORE

My nose woke up my stomach before the rest of my body even had a chance. By the time I got my eyes open I was officially starving.

The air was full of the smell of coffee and something spicy and rich.

The wide white plane of Jack's bed was empty, the blankets tossed back on his side. I'd slept so hard I barely moved. I tossed aside the covers and looked over the edge of the bed to see his dress shirt still in a heap on the floor. Smiling to myself, I slipped it on and then followed the smells to find Jack.

The condo was a surprise in the bright light of day. Hardwood floors, simple but nice furniture, little to no decorations except for the books. So many books. In shelves, in stacks against the wall, propped open on his big brown leather couch.

The books made me feel safe; they reminded me of

my sister.

I stepped into the kitchen and found him standing at the stove, wearing a pair of flannel pajama pants and his tattoos and nothing else.

And he was perfect. Mouthwateringly so. That he stood here, half-naked in this beautiful bizarre apartment, made me feel like he was showing me a secret, telling me something he did not tell anyone else, and the enormity of it was disarming.

"Hey," I said, standing in the doorway, feeling shy.

Feeling utterly unlike myself in any way.

Like the scene was familiar but I didn't know my part or my lines. So I had to wing it.

I had to be myself, and I didn't know who that was right now.

"Hey," he said, glancing over his shoulder at me, and then hilariously doing a double take. "Wow... that look, no wonder it's in all the movies."

"The shirt?" I ran my fingers along the buttons. This was a good look on most women, but killer on me.

"Mostly you. But a little bit the shirt. Coffee?"

"I'd love some."

His kitchen was lovely. White tile and black appliances. He had copper pots hanging from a peg board along one wall. He poured me a cup of coffee and set it on the island in the middle of the room.

"Sugar is there," he said, pointing to a little pot on the island. "Milk?"

"I just take sugar." I doctored my coffee and leaned against the island to watch him. It was awkward, a little. More than what I usually felt the morning after, but not enough to make me get dressed and leave.

"What's your last name?" I asked.

He blinked at me. "Herrara. You?"

"Blakely."

"You feel like we should have done that before we had sex?" he asked.

I tried to pretend to be easy. Comfortable, but he wasn't buying it. "Maybe."

"You feel like this was a mistake?"

I shook my head but then I said, "Maybe."

He put his hand through his hair, making the curls stand on end, and then he turned toward me with so much somber focus I sat up straight, startled.

"Today is Sunday," he said and I nodded as if confirming, yes indeed. Today is Sunday.

"I have the next few days off. I go back Wednesday." I nodded again, as if committing the timeline to memory.

"I can take you home, anytime. Anytime at all. Call you a cab. Drive you myself, whatever you want. You can leave and not tell me. You can—"

I smiled, feeling so tender toward his earnest appeal. "I'm free to go anytime. You've made that clear."

"But… you could stay until Wednesday morning. If you wanted. You could stay here with me."

"What would we do?" I asked, because really, there was no question that I would stay.

"Well, I imagine I'll feed you and then I'll fuck you. And we'll just keep repeating that."

"Sounds charming."

"It's not. It won't be."

The smile fell from my face. The fire in my body he seemed to control with just a look reignited.

"What happens Wednesday morning?" I asked, though I knew.

"It's over. It's over like it never happened. You walk out the door and we can't see each other again. Ever. You can't call or text. Or stop by the club. Nothing. Do you understand that?"

"Over like it never happened," I repeated, tasting the bitter edge of those words. "On Wednesday."

He nodded, his arms braced on the kitchen island, all those muscles in relief against the tattoos.

"Three days," I said.

"Three days."

Some sensible part of my brain was trying to remind me that who he was and what he did wasn't a fucking joke.

It wasn't.

And I couldn't pretend like what he did wasn't real, because it was as real as that gun of his. And the blood that had been on his face.

But it just felt so far away right now.

And three days felt like that diner last night. A bright island of light in a sea of darkness.

And if it was going to be over in three days…

"Are we supposed to shake on it?" I asked, smiling at him, because he needed to be smiled at, and frankly, I needed him to smile again. "My sister and I always pinky promised." I held out my pinky for him to link his to. But he surprised me by grabbing my hand and pressing his lips to my knuckles.

"Three days," he breathed. Like I'd done far more than just agree to let him feed me and fuck me for hours in a row. "You won't regret it."

Well, I wasn't sure about that. Something told me I'd be thinking about the next three days when I was old and gray.

"What are you making me for breakfast?" I asked.

"*Chiliquiles*. Mom used to make them for my brother and me on special mornings."

"Old family recipe?" I joked.

"Something like that. Give me a second." He broke two eggs over a hot frying pan, and while they fried he filled a plate with tortillas, spooned green sauce over them from a pot on his stove. Broke up fresh white cheese over that, and then finally slipped the eggs over all of it.

My stomach roared again.

"I can't believe I didn't feed you last night," he said, bringing the plate over to the island.

"If that tastes as good as that looks you are forgiven."

He smiled at me, shy again as he turned the plate so it looked like I got the best side. I dug in with the fork he handed me and at the first taste I closed my eyes and moaned.

"You are completely forgiven."

He ducked his head and dug into the plate between us.

"Do you cook a lot?" I asked, looking over at his wall of pots.

"No. Not much. Those were my mom's. When she died I couldn't bear to throw them away."

I stared at him, mouth agape.

"What?" he asked. "Is that so weird?"

Rare, I thought. Extraordinary. Special. I could say all those things, but we were in this light space between us, smiling over food he made.

And none of it mattered after Wednesday morning.

"Yes," I said, deadpan. "Very weird."

Everything about this man was not what I thought. Was nothing like what I expected.

I sighed and tilted my head, gazing at his arms, the tattoos in all their violent glory. I reached out and traced with my finger the thick vein that traveled from his wrist up the side of his forearm, past a vicious angel with a bloody sword in one hand, and a bleeding red heart in the other.

"Vengeance?"

"Justice."

A chill ran down my body, but this was the cost of being with him. It was pleasure laced with fear. It was desire dark with the unknown.

And in my safe, small little life I found him... addictive and I wanted more. So much more.

My finger cupped his arm, the thick swell of his bicep, covered in Spanish words.

"What's it say?"

"The sins of the father." His breath caught and shuddered as I stepped closer, my fingers now on his collarbone, the hard ridge of it. My heartbeat pounded between my legs.

"What are these?" I asked, touching numbers on his ribcage.

"The day my mother died. And the day my father died."

"And this one?"

It was 500,000.

"Nothing," he said, shifting his body so that tattoo

was blocked.

I glanced up at him, surprised he would lie. Because he was so clearly lying.

"I can't... I can't tell you everything," he said. "There are things I just—" He swallowed and I understood. There were things he couldn't say out loud, for my sake or his.

"Take off your pants," I whispered and he blinked at me, as if surprised. But then he did it, shucking them in no time. I nearly smiled.

"Take off my shirt," he said and I went to work on the five buttons I'd done up, but apparently that was taking too long because he grabbed the two sides of the shirt and tore it open.

I screamed and then laughed, shrugging out of the ripped shirt, and so we stood there in front of each other in the bright light of a new day falling through the windows across our skin.

I looked my fill, knowing he was doing the same. Seeing imperfections I couldn't hide with makeup or lighting, and I didn't care.

He was so beautiful like this. Naked and vulnerable and I could tell in his stillness he found me beautiful like this too.

So I pulled myself up onto the island, the tiles cold against my butt and thighs, and my movement had the predictable effect of making him look at me.

I spread my legs a little for him. Shook my hair off my shoulders.

"I want to come," I said. A privileged demand.

"Fuck," he breathed, coming up against my body, his hips between my thighs. His hands on my back, running along my spine, making me curl into him.

"How?" he asked. "How would my princess like to come?"

He kissed my nipple, sucking it into his mouth, his tongue sweeping over it and then he let it go, blowing against the damp skin until I moaned.

"You want to come against my hand?" he asked and pulled my other nipple into his mouth. Licking it until it was hard and I was wet. "My cock?"

"Your mouth."

Oh, his eyes. The blaze of heat there, the smirk on his lips. It was crazy how they made me feel. Like a stranger to myself in some ways. Like he'd opened up some secret room of desire inside of me.

"Whatever my princess desires," he whispered and he pulled my hips closer to the edge of the counter and then fell to his knees in front of me.

I didn't feel the cold tiles, the sunlight, the draft from some open window. I felt nothing but the bright hot sweep of his tongue against my body.

I flinched as his tongue hit my clit, moaned as he went back again and again.

He mapped me with his mouth, a slow and sweet exploration of every secret place. Every fold. He found the spots that made me twitch, that made me clench my hands in his silky hair. He found those spots and he made them his. He worked me and stroked me. He licked me and tongued me.

I was wet and he was wet and he had my ass in his hands, and every time I twitched away, he pulled me closer. Not letting me off any hook. Not letting me shrink away from any moment of this.

It was wild and messy and the most unrestrained thing I'd ever been a part of. Men had gone down on me before—but not like this. Not like I was a treasure. A feast to be devoured.

In the end I put one hand around his head, holding him to me as he sucked on my clit. My other hand falling back against the counter as I tried to keep myself upright.

"Yes," I breathed. "Yes. Oh God. Oh fuck."

He slipped a finger inside of me. Curled it up until he found the place that made me scream, and it was too much. I pulled away again, trying to shove his head away, but he was stronger and he was unrelenting and I came so hard I fell backward, throwing the plate off the counter. I jerked against him, the orgasm going on and on until I thought I was having another one, and then I was.

I'd never come so much or so hard, and I felt out-side of myself. Like I'd blacked out and when I opened my eyes he was standing up between my legs, which I could barely feel.

"You okay?" he asked.

"I knocked… I knocked something over."

It was a ridiculous thing to say. I felt like I'd come so hard I'd lost a leg or something. I couldn't feel parts of my body.

"You've done some damage," he said, but he wasn't talking about his plate. Or the mess on the other side of the island.

"Good," I said and leaned forward and kissed him, pulling his lip into my mouth, biting it.

He pulled me up and I wrapped my arms around his neck and my legs around his waist and he took me back into the bedroom where we made love like it was all going to end the second we stopped touching.

So we didn't stop.

"WHAT'S THE DEAL with economics?" I asked. I didn't know what day it was. Only that it was dark again and we'd gobbled up Chinese food hours ago. We were on his couch, I was lying in his arms, my hands tracing the dark outline of the crown of thorns on the inside of his elbow. Three of the thorns had blood on them.

"Like why did I pick it?" he asked.

"Yeah."

"I'm not sure I remember," he said.

I pinched him and he squeezed me tighter in his arms. "Think back so long ago. Five whole years…"

"I was planning on being an accountant," he said and kissed my hair. "Money and my family was always a disaster. Like every day my parents' worry about having it and making it and keeping it and trying to make more—it was this black cloud. And being an accountant seemed like the best job I could think of to not just make money, but I could also deal with this black cloud of worry in my house."

"Your dad—"

He shook his head.

"What?"

"I don't… No talking about my dad. I don't… I don't want him here. With you."

I felt the bite of tears behind my eyes and I had to look away.

I kissed the inside of his elbow, the crown of thorns.

"That's why you scolded me about credit card debt and the Uber?" I finally managed to say. That I found that adorable was slightly disturbing.

"Old habits I guess," he said.

"How'd you go from accounting to economics?"

"I took Intro to Economics, and we studied this guy

Alfred Marshall and he said this thing about money and man, and it just…it blew my mind."

"What did he say?"

"'Economics is a study of man in the ordinary business of life. Thus, it is on the one side, the study of wealth and on the other and more important side, a part of the study of man.'"

I rolled over so I was facing him, my legs parting over his hips. The soft warm center of my body settling against him in a way he clearly liked.

"Say it again," I said, wrapping my arms around his neck. Kissing his ear.

He laughed. "You like that? A little dirty economics talk?"

"Yeah." I took his ear lobe in between my teeth. "Give me more of that filthy economics, baby."

"How about this," he whispered, his wide hands sweeping up my back to my hair and back down again. "'Economics is the science which traces the laws of society as arise from the combined operations of mankind for the production of wealth, in so far as those phenomena are not modified by the pursuit of any other object.'"

I wiggled against him, pressing my breast to his chest so I could feel him breathing and the soft happy gust of his laughter. "Say phenomena again," I whispered.

His hands boosted under my ass and he put his feet on the ground and stood up, holding me like it was nothing. Like it was easy.

And it was easy. It was easy in these three days to be these people. I couldn't say who we were, who I was.

But it was remarkably easy.

"You are a phenomenon," he said, taking me to the bedroom and laying me out across his bed. And I came under his hands, his fingers and his body. Never in my life had I come so easily, like my body was simply waiting for him to arrive and show me what I could do.

CHAPTER NINE

Abby

BEFORE

HOURS LATER, THE middle of the night, maybe—I couldn't know, like we'd decided to ignore time, while being so tightly tuned to it. Aware, every passing minute that we were ticking toward our end.

I texted Charlotte because we hadn't not spoken for so long in our lives. And I had about a thousand texts from her that I hadn't answered and she was getting agitated.

Hey.

Jesus, she texted back almost immediately. *Where are you? Are you literally locked in a closet?*

No. I texted. *I'm actually in the opposite of a closet.*

Everything okay?

At the moment yes. But I'm going to need to cry on your shoulder soon enough.

You're freaking me out.

I'm okay. I love you. I'll call Wednesday night.

I went back Jack's dark bedroom and climbed under the blankets, finding my way to his body by touch.

"Day drunk is the best drunk," I said, handing him the bottle of tequila.

"Especially Monday day drunk," he said.

"Monday day drunk is wrong in all the right ways," I said.

"So wrong. Dirty, even." He shifted, kissing my foot where it was balanced on his arm, and water sloshed over the edge of the bath.

"Careful," I said, but he didn't care. The bathroom was practically a lake. This bath was the best idea.

He handed me the tequila, but I didn't drink. My head was already swimming. "Can I ask you something?"

"You can." He nodded. "I can't promise I'll answer."

"What's the story with church?" I asked.

"Like the history of it?"

"No, funny guy. What's your story with church?"

"All right. You can't tell anyone."

"Oh, this should be good." I sat up, sending a little wave over the white porcelain edge of the tub. He lifted his hand for the tequila and I handed it over.

"Before economics, when I was a little kid, I wanted to be a priest."

I gaped at him. Mouth dropped open.

He leaned forward and shut my jaw with his fingers, his thumb slipping over my lip. I opened my mouth and let him come in, just a little.

"My mom was so devout," he said. "And because she went so often and it was such a big part of her life, I believed that she loved it. And so I loved it. She… I don't think actually loved it. I think she just needed forgiveness and strength and guidance."

"Why?" I breathed.

"My father was… a difficult man."

I held my breath, waiting to see if he would break his rule from hours earlier, but he said no more about his father.

"What made you change your mind?" I asked. "About being a priest."

"Melissa Cummings," he said. Suddenly he reached forward and grabbed me by my hips, pulling me up into his lap.

Water everywhere.

"Yeah?" I asked, twining wet soapy arms around his neck. "What did Melissa do?"

He licked my breast, pulling my nipple into his mouth, I sighed against him.

"She let me do this," he said, licking his way over to my other breast. I rocked against him, his erection slipping between my legs. Heat coiled through me. I'd spent the last hours in a constant state of simmer. Ready for him.

I reached between us, my hand cupping one side of his cock, the other side of his cock pressed up against me. Not inside me, just against me. Where I was hot and wet.

He hissed and I liked that sound so much I made him do it again.

"I want to fuck you," he said against my neck, shifting as if to get up with me in his arms

"No," I said, because I liked the power. And I liked his cock against my clit and his mouth against my breast.

"You don't want me to fuck you?" he said. He sucked the skin of my neck into his mouth and I was covered with these little bruises. Little love bites. Marked like an animal.

"Not right now," I breathed. "I want you to come like this."

He leaned back, his eyes burning in the white tiled bathroom. "Dangerous," he breathed. "You are so fucking dangerous."

I grinned, because I knew it. Because I loved it.

And I made him rut against me like he was an animal.

And I loved that too.

"I TOLD YOU something I never told anyone," he said, hours later. He was making me dinner. Which was leftover Chinese food. That had been our breakfast too. I was beginning to think I could live the rest of my life in this condo, eating leftover beef and broccoli. I sat on his kitchen island, drinking a glass of wine. Monday day drunk was turning into Monday evening drunk. Which was all right with me. Everything was all right with me.

"Melissa Cummings?"

"No. Wanting to be a priest."

"Well, it was very hot pretending to defrock you."

The skin of his neck turned pink and blotchy when he was embarrassed. It was very endearing. I wanted to kiss the edges of that blush, the place where the pink skin faded into pale.

"Tell me something," he said, bringing over the plate of spicy eggplant. "Something you haven't told anyone."

"I wanted to be a priest too. You should pretend to defrock me."

"I will. Later." He dug into his fried rice and I sat on his island, the eggplant cooling off on my plate. I was going to tell him, it was clear that I was. I just had to open my mouth and the words would come out. Like they'd been waiting for this moment.

For him.

In this wide world, I felt like I never fit. Only with my sister did I fall into some kind of place. But in my life, I was always just missing real connections, floating past people. Perhaps it was the chemistry thing and how I could manipulate it. Maybe it was because I had my sister and everyone else was second to that.

Maybe I was just an asshole, I had no idea.

But I fit with Jack. Like a worn puzzle piece, I fit him. And he fit me. And I'd never felt this before.

"I'm saving money to open a café."

There. The dream. Out in the open.

"Really?" He nodded, like that made sense.

"I've been saving money for like three years."

"To open your own place?"

"Yeah." I poked at the eggplant with my fork. "My first job after high school was at this café run by this French woman, and it was really beautiful. She had coffee and pastries and beautiful platters of salads that she made fresh every day, and in the afternoon she sold wine and beer and people would come in and stay all day working on laptops. Or moms would come in with their babies. Or couples would meet there after dinner for a glass of wine. And her daughter would come there after school, and her husband met her there after work. It was like this... oasis in the neighborhood. And I loved it. I loved how everyone knew everyone. How all these appetites and needs were met in one place and she was orchestrating all of it. She was giving everyone what they needed."

"Sounds beautiful," he said.

"It was. It probably still is. But I was young and I wanted to make more money and be a sexy party girl I guess, so I left after a few months, but I… well, I never forgot that. And a few years ago I started to want something else for myself it kind of became all I could think of."

"So you want to open a café like that one?"

"I have some ideas of my own, but yeah… yes. I want to open my own place. I want to give everyone what they need under one roof."

"That's a good dream," he said. "How much money do you have?"

"Not enough. Not if I want to do it in San Francisco and…" I shook my head. "I don't even know if I can do it, you know? I'm so shit at bank stuff and payroll and budgets. Like, I'd fuck it up before I even got it started. It's stupid, really a dumb—"

He kissed me, stopping my words with his mouth.

"What are you doing?" I laughed, wiping his lips and my lips. We tasted like each other and oyster sauce.

He grabbed our plates and set them down on the tiled island. "Defrocking you."

I WOKE UP to the extra loud bings of a series of texts coming into my phone, and cursing I rolled over and grabbed it before the sound woke Jack up.

The texts were from a phone number I didn't know, and instead of turning off the phone and going back to sleep against Jack's back, my cheek nestled against his spine, I looked at the text.

> *This is Bates from the Moonlight. We'd like to talk to you about a management position at the club. After the other night Patty has been promoted to Manager and you would be working with her. Mr. Lazarus would like to meet you to discuss this in person. Notify me of your interest.*

I rolled over in Jack's bed, staring at the text. My heart high in my throat. Management position? Me?

"Everything okay?" he asked, kissing my shoulder. There was not a single part of my body he had not touched, kissed, laid his tongue upon. I was covered in him, just as he was covered in me.

"Did I wake you?" I asked.

He shook his head, his curly hair tickly against my shoulder.

"Patty got promoted at the Moonlight," I told him.

"That's smart," he said and then cracked his jaw open in a giant yawn. "She text you?"

"Bates did."

He went stone cold still against me, and I made the mistake of turning to look at him. To see his rigid face, the face I hadn't seen since the first night I met him. It was scary, that face, here in his bed, in this safe place that smelled of our bodies.

"What did he say?" he asked through lips that barely moved.

"He wants to talk to me about a job."

He got out of the bed, pulling on the flannel pants crumpled on the floor. He was furious, and I knew enough that his anger was really fear in disguise. And the fear was for me.

"Jack—"

"How does he even fucking have your number?"

"I don't know?"

"Delete the text and block the number."

"Please calm down—"

"Abby. You can't work there."

"That's not your call!" I yelled, mostly because he was yelling at me and not letting me finish a goddamn sentence. I mean, I understood he was scared, but he couldn't talk to me like this.

And frankly, I was pleased in a way to get this offer. Couldn't I have that? Couldn't I just have a minute with this?

"Do you think I get this kind of opportunity every day?" I asked.

"Opportunity? Are you crazy?"

"Don't be mean!"

"You deserve so much better than the Moonlight."

That took some of the wind out of my angry sails and I sagged in the bed. His sheets pulled over my breasts.

"I'm not," I whispered with a kind of bone-chilling honesty, "very good at knowing what I deserve."

He left the doorway to crouch in front of me at the end of the bed. "What do you think you deserve?"

I blinked at him, stunned maybe by the question, having never heard it before. *What did I deserve? Who determines that? Who decides such a thing?*

"I don't even know how to answer that."

"Can I tell you what I think you deserve?"

Oh God, this was too much. Too much. I felt like my heart was somehow in his hands. Like he was looking directly into my cringing self-confidence buried beneath all my bravado. He was looking at the young me, the sick me, the scared me, the dumb me.

And he didn't blink. He didn't glance away.

He could tear me apart with whatever he was going to say. He could wound me so much worse than I could wound myself.

I wanted to turn away from this intimacy. I wanted to say something flip or kiss him just to distract him, but somehow despite all those inclinations I said:

"Yes."

"I think you deserve a job you love, that uses all your skills, not just your looks and your ability to read people. I think you deserve to try something hard just so you can see yourself succeed. I think you deserve to see yourself the way that I see you."

My breath left me in a shaky exhale. I tried to turn my face aside but he touched my chin, holding me still with the warmth of his fingertips against my skin. My bone.

"How do you see me?"

"Fully fucking capable of doing whatever you want."

I curled my arms around Jack's shoulders. Hugging his neck, his warm bare skin all along my warm bare skin. We felt like velvet together.

We felt just right.

"What do you think you deserve?" I asked into his shoulder. He stilled, so quick. So totally, I wasn't sure he was breathing. It was as if he'd even stopped his heart.

But then he twitched away from me and I held on tight.

"Don't," he said.

"It's just a question."

"No. It's not, and you know that." He grabbed my hands, peeling them from around his neck, putting distance between us by force.

"Can I tell you what I think you deserve?"

"Abby—"

He stood and I stood up too, but he kept a foot of distance between us when I tried to get closer. He finally put his hand up between us, his palm against my chest.

"Abby, stop."

"I can't, Jack. I can't stop. I don't know what happened that made you get into this life you're living. I don't know who or what you're protecting, but you deserve so much more. So much better."

He stepped toward me, grabbing my shoulders, lifting me up on to my toes. "You know why I have these days off?" he asked. "All this time to fuck you and play house?"

"Jack—"

"Because I put a man in the hospital, Abby. I broke him so bad a machine is breathing for him. He's eating through a tube. I am lying low from his crew and from the cops. And the only reasons I'm not in jail or dead is because he's unconscious and because he deserved it."

"No," I breathed.

"I am punishment, Abby. I am the fucking hand of Lazarus, and if I walk in your door it's because I am going to hurt you so bad you will never forget it and because you deserve the pain I give you."

Tears flooded my eyes, spilling over my cheeks.

"Jack," I whispered, reaching for him. But he put me down on my feet and pushed me away, smacking at my hands as I tried to touch him. "Jack. That's not you."

"Not me? You are stupid, aren't you?"

I flinched but said nothing.

"What is wrong with you?" he asked, sneering at me. "What is wrong with you that you still want me? Don't you fucking get it? You should run away from me."

"I don't know what happened between the boy who joined the wrestling team for his brother and who you are now, but something happened."

"You're filling in the blanks, princess." He shook his head at me like I was such a disappointment. "Believing what you want. I thought you were fucking smarter than that." He said it like I was such a disappointment, and I knew what he was doing and it still hurt.

"I care about you," I said, as stark and honest as I could be.

"Stop."

"I care about you." I stepped toward him.

"Abby."

"I care about you and I think you care about me."

He turned toward me again, his eyes glittering, his lips split into a snarl so mean it nearly sliced through my skin. He was coming for me. He was coming to hurt me. And I would take it because I deserved him.

The truth of him. The reality of him. The floppy hair, shy smile, apartment full of books.

And he deserved me, wanting and trying and vulnerable.

We deserved each other—this, what he was going to do right now, was just noise.

I was in. I was so deep and so far into this man, I couldn't find my way out even if I wanted to.

He charged toward me, stopping when our chests touched and I gasped at the contact, relieved even though I knew he was going to hurt me. Not physically, but emotionally. He was going to try and tear me apart right now, because I told him how I felt.

"Don't make up fairytales about me, princess," he said, his voice hard.

"You're too late," I said. "You're too late for everything. I see you, Jack. I want you."

He pushed me back on the bed and I fell, my legs akimbo, my hand smacking into the books on the bedside table.

"You don't know me," he said, lip curled like I was disgusting. But his cock was hard beneath the flannel pajamas. I put my arms over my head, curling my body so he saw all the best parts. The parts he liked the most. My breasts, my wrists, the bones of my hips. My spreading thighs.

"Don't I?" I asked.

I dropped one hand between my legs, lifting my knees so I could touch myself while he watched. "I know you like this," I breathed, showing him the pink of me. The heat and damp of me. "I know you want this," I said, circling my clit with my fingernail, while he watched, mesmerized. Poor boy, I thought, to be so torn. "You want it, don't you?" I asked.

"Yes," he hissed.

"It's yours, Jack."

Still, he stood there.

"Take it," I said.

He pushed down his pants and crawled onto the bed between my legs. The mattress dipped beneath me and I tilted toward him. I lifted my hips, the soft damp edges of my pussy stroking him. My fingers stroking him.

"You don't scare me," I said.

He grabbed my hands, pinning them to the bed, but I stared up at him defiant. Turned on. My body his.

"It's too late," I warned him. "I've seen you. I know you."

"You don't." His voice was hard, the words spat into my face, and for a moment I wavered. "You know what I want you to know. And that's it."

I shook my head, smiling into his anger. Forgiving him even as he tried to scare me. I lifted my hips again and then shifted him so he slid just inside of my body.

An inch of his cock inside me.

He growled. Snarled. My sweet shy lover from the last few days got eaten by this wolf I didn't recognize.

"I know you," I said, stroking him with my body. Squeezing him, taking more and more of him even as he would resist me. "I know the real you."

He used one hand to hold both my hands and his other palm cupped my neck. My throat. I lifted my chin, inviting the pressure.

Lifting my hips, fucking him even as he would not fuck me.

"I should scare you," he said, squeezing my throat. A warning. A bite of fear. My body ran hot and wet. I was in utter surrender under him. "I should scare the fuck out of you."

I smiled at him, showing him my teeth. Showing him my ferocity.

For a second his hand squeezed and his body coiled.

"Don't lie to yourself, princess," he said. "Don't love me."

I didn't say it, but I didn't have to: *Too late.*

"Do your worst," I said instead, and he ducked his head and thrust so hard into me I screamed. He eased out and did it again, shoving himself inside of me like it was punishment, but I was wet and ready and it felt so good I could cry.

"I want to remember you like this," he said, thrusting into me again. My whole body arched under him, held to the bed only by his hips and his hand at my throat. My arms came up over his back, holding us together, but he shook me off and pulled out of me.

"What—" I gasped, disoriented by the sudden emptiness of my body. He flipped me over, lifted me to my knees, and I braced one hand against the wall, knowing what was coming.

I bit my lip as he thrust into me, I bit my lip so hard and he fucked me so hard I saw stars and the pressure inside my body grew and grew until it was almost too much.

"You want to come?" he asked.

"Yes."

He stopped moving, curled over my back. "Beg me. Beg me to make you come, princess."

I dropped my hand from the wall and reached for my clit, but he smacked my hand away. "Me," he said.

"Please," I moaned. "Make me come."

He thrust again. Hard and sure and then his fingers instead of reaching for my clit, circled my asshole. I screamed, wanting to come up on my toes.

The pressure in my clit painful now. My whole body hurt with the need to come. He braced his legs wide and his other hand came around to rub at my clit and I exploded.

"Fuck yes," he moaned against my back. "Yes, just like that."

I was coming. I was coming so hard it came down my legs, it covered his hand. "You," I moaned, putting my sweaty head down on the bed.

"What?"

"Come. Please, Jack. Come inside me."

I was boneless under him, a thing for him to move and shift into whatever position felt good to him, and I'd never felt so connected to someone. I'd never felt so powerful and rewarded, and part of me in the back of my brain where I could still think in words thought with wonder that this was only the beginning.

He came with a cry and a shaking thrust that flattened us both onto the bed. A sweaty messy lump.

I felt him breathing over me, the beat of his heart pounding into my back. I could feel him thinking, and his thoughts were dark and sharp.

"I'm okay," I said, because I knew he was worried. Scared he'd been too rough when he'd been perfect.

Instead of relaxing, he only got more stiff. He pulled out of me and I hid my wince, because I knew he would think I was hurt when I was only sore.

"I'm... shit... Abby?"

"What?"

"We didn't use a condom."

CHAPTER TEN

Abby

BEFORE

I ROLLED OVER and faced him, but he sat on the side of the bed, his back to me, his head bowed. A bright fissure of panic crackled through me.

"I'm clean," I said.

"So am I." Our voices were quiet like we were in a hospital. Or at a funeral. "I give blood at church every month," he said and looked at me over his shoulder.

"I believe you," I told him, because I knew what he needed from me at that moment. Calm and faith. I knew what he needed because I needed the same damn thing.

"And if you're pregnant—"

"I'm on the pill."

But my pills were at home. I hadn't taken one since Saturday morning. Shit. It was Monday night. Fuck. Charlotte got on me about this all the time. ALL THE TIME. She was going to kill me. But I never had sex without a condom. Never. This was a total first for me.

Jack was a total first for me in every way.

"I'll get the morning after pill," I told him. Even though Maria had gotten pregnant after taking the morning after pill. Oh God, what had I done?

"But if you're pregnant," he said, "I'd like to know."

"It's my choice, whatever happens." I sounded more scared than I was. I think.

"I know. I agree. And I won't stand in the way of whatever you do. But... I'd like to help you. Money or whatever."

"Whatever?" I asked, pulling at something I knew I shouldn't. Not if I wanted him to get back into this bed with me. "Like, you'll hold my hand at the clinic? Bring me home? Or go to the doctor's appointments with me? Birthing classes."

"Abby," he sighed, like I was just asking so much. And I was, in a way—we barely knew each other. But at the same time, this thing had happened between us. This potential catastrophe. My nerves were twitching inside my skin.

And like he saw that, he reached out and touched my hair, stroked the skin of my shoulder. "Whatever happens," he said. "It will be okay."

"Yeah? How is that possible with your three day rule?"

He had no answer. None.

He got up, the pale skin of his ass and thighs glowing in the dim room. "I'll be back," he said.

I fell asleep waiting for him. Cold in his warm bed.

I WOKE UP again to his side of the bed empty. My purse was on the bottom of the bed as well as my clothes, all folded into a stack. My leggings replaced by the pair of his sweatpants I'd been wearing while I'd been here.

I sighed at the sight.

The air was empty of delicious smells and the condo was silent. Cold.

I hung my head for a moment, hurt more than I thought I could be by a man I both barely knew and felt like I knew down to the ground.

But it would seem we had crossed a line for him, and now he was going to clean that up by asking me to leave.

My body ached as I got out of bed, and I could see on my wrists and breasts the lingering signs of our last twenty-four hours. Beard burns and bruises, red marks. My body was an artifact. And I treasured every twinge and sore spot as I pulled on my clothes.

I gathered up my stuff, gave myself one last look in the mirror, and tried to tell myself I didn't care.

But it was all a lie.

The sight of him in his kitchen, surrounded by his copper pots, back in his suit, the deep black of it like a hole ripped in the rosiness of the last few days. It was ugly, that suit. A harsh reminder of things I did not want to be reminded of.

And if the suit wasn't enough of an indicator that he was getting rid of me, his face made it clear.

Handsome as sin, cold to the bone. He looked at me like he'd never touched me. Like he'd never begged me. Like I hadn't tasted his come and he hadn't tasted mine.

"Good morning," I said, the chill of the tile floors seeping up into my feet. Creeping up my legs. The apartment had been so warm for so long, now the chill was everywhere and—as he turned his midnight eyes to me—I knew it was coming from him.

On the counter in front of him was a small box from a pharmacy.

"I got this for you," he said. The morning after pill. He pushed it toward me and I picked it up with shaking hands.

"I've also called you a car," he said, his voice hard. "It's time for you to go."

"What day is it?" I asked.

"It doesn't matter."

"You're kicking me out because of last night. Because it was a little too real for you."

He got to his feet so fast I held my breath, unsure of what he would do. But he just walked to the sink, got out a glass, and filled it with water like that was all that mattered.

"Fuck you, Jack. You're not fooling me with this act."

"Jesus Christ." His voice was a sneer and I braced myself for him to say something awful. To try and hurt me enough to leave. "You're not that special, Abby. In fact, there are hundreds of girls like you in this city. Beautiful, dumb—"

I flinched and he stopped. Knowing what he was doing didn't make it hurt less. Tears, a steady threat since waking up and seeing my bag at the bottom of the bed, flooded my eyes and I turned my face aside, wiping one away in hopes he wouldn't see it.

But he saw it. And he did nothing.

And part of me wanted to smack his face and leave. And maybe I'd still do that. But part of me saw exactly what he was doing. The cage he'd built around himself was shrinking every day, and this was how he protected himself.

"When I was a kid—"

"I don't care," he lied.

"Fuck you, Jack!" I snapped. "You'll listen to me because you owe me that. And you do fucking care and I'm going to leave, don't worry, but let's not fucking lie to each other now." He was silent, holding onto the edge of the counter like it was the only thing he had. I held onto my purse the same way. Like it was hold onto something as hard as I could, or fall to pieces. "My parents took Charlotte and me to this dude ranch in Idaho, way out in the middle of nowhere. It was a total one-off, but Char and I were getting older, and I was getting into some boy trouble while my sister was retreating inside her room more and more, and I think my parents saw this as a chance to get us together as a family."

I glanced up at him, and then away because he was staring at me so intently it was like he was looking inside my head. My skin. He could see my beating heart.

I saw him think: *That's why, that night in the car, at the very beginning, you said you'd go to Idaho.*

And I let him see me think: *Yes, Sherlock. Now listen.*

"Charlotte got sick, like… right away. Some kind of stomach thing and she couldn't leave our cabin, which frankly suited her fine. She's like you, she brought seven thousand books with her to read. I think that's why I felt so safe with you. Or felt like I knew you when I didn't. Why I still feel that way." I stopped, cleared my throat, and forced myself back on topic. "Anyway, Mom was taking care of her and Dad—well, Dad never had much to do with us. We didn't have much to do with him. I expected to hate it. There were no parties, no shopping. No cell phone service. My friends felt a million miles away. The closest town was this place called Silver Falls, and it had like a bar and a café and seven hundred churches and that was it. I was prepared to pitch a fit every day until we went home. But... I loved it. I loved it like it was mine. Like it fit me. And I fit it." I laughed, remembering how surprising it was to love something like I loved that vacation. That weird little dude ranch. "The family that ran it let me work with the horses every day, and I got to eat with all the staff at this big table, and the cook let me help in the kitchen one day, and it felt like all the work I was doing was important. It felt... it felt like I was important."

He made some noise in his throat like he under-stood, like he understood even what I wasn't saying. Didn't know how to say about how empty my life was and how I needed purpose.

"And I know I was a kid, and I know they were humoring me, but it was real to me. And I've never felt that way again until—"

"Abby. Don't."

"You make me feel important. You fit me. And I fit you and this is going to suck, because you can't change that, Jack. It just is."

He went to the door and started unlocking the locks.

"Don't do this," I said, begging in a way I never

thought I would. "Don't make me leave."

"It's already done. You are already gone."

The man I'd spent the last two days with was not here, and I could see I wasn't going to get him back. There was nothing he would hear.

Silent, I took my barely restrained tears and my trembling anger and bruised body and began the process of peeling myself from this place. From this man. Before I got to the doorknob he stepped slightly into my way and I recoiled, terrified he would touch me and terrified I would shatter at the sensation.

"If you're pregnant, you call me."

"No."

He couldn't even look me in the eye. I watched as he swallowed. His Adam's apple bobbing as if he was choking something awful down. "Call me," he said. "Please."

I leaned in, as close as I could. So close I could smell him, and he smelled like I did. We smelled like each other. And his bed would smell like us. His sheets and pillows. His whole house was covered in me and he was going to have to live here.

"Goodbye, Jack," I said. I left his apartment without giving him any promises and without looking back.

I ignored whatever car he might have ordered for me and walked toward the large intersection I could see down the hill. I needed air and I needed movement and I needed to exercise the ghosts of Jack from my body. Holding up his sweatpants, I started to run. Sprint.

Pushing him out of my muscles and skin.

My heart chugged and my lungs screamed and I ran until my brain let go of the thought of him. Just for the moment. For the now.

And it was enough.

I got to the intersection and realized I wasn't that far from my house. Another mile. Maybe a bit more, and I pressed on. Running until I was dripping in sweat.

All the way home in my too-big sweatpants and my bag banging against my shoulder, I ran because to stop would let him back in.

Once in my apartment, the door slammed shut behind me, I wanted to collapse on the floor, but I didn't. I went to the sink and took the pill and then I shed my clothes and walked right into the shower, where I shampooed the smell of his shampoo out of my hair and I ran hands over my body, ignoring the marks he left on me.

Because they would fade.

Just like the memories.

It was nothing, I told myself. It was a moment. The appeal was the surprise of him. The perceived danger. The mystery.

It was the fact that I filled all the blanks in my knowledge with something noble or kind, when the truth was I had so little to back that up.

I'd convinced myself by the time I got out of the shower that he was only special because of the mystery. He was only special because I made him that way.

I wrapped myself in my favorite robe and went back to my bag to pull out my makeup and throw my dirty clothes in the laundry.

At the bottom of the bag, beneath the sparkly gold dress, something rustled. I pulled out the sweaty and terrible wrinkled work dress and the shoes and there at the bottom of my bag were stacks of papers.

"What in the world?"

Flipping through them, I realized they were all the restaurant spaces for lease or sale in the Bay area.

He'd printed them off for me at some point while I was sleeping. And then put them in the bottom of the bag so I wouldn't see them until I got home.

Tears burned behind my eyes.

And despite all my brave words, I fell down to my knees at the foot of my bed and sobbed.

CHAPTER ELEVEN

Abby

BEFORE

I WENT BACK to work two days later. Sun, Maria, and I were selling tequila at a fancy Mexican restaurant. We wore black dresses and bright red lipstick and the money was good.

"Hey," Sun said one night after work. "Want to go out tonight?"

"It's midnight, Sun," I said, through a yawn.

"Night's just getting started. There's a band playing down at the HiLo."

I shook my head, exhausted. Exhausted by work. Exhausted by pretending to be okay. Exhausted by trying not to think of Jack and then failing. And failing. And failing.

The failure not to think about Jack was killing me.

He was killing me.

The memory of his hands. Of his smile. The tilt of his chin in the tub as he drank. The rumble of his chest under my ear as he laughed, telling me dirty economic jokes. These things snuck up on me like ghosts in the night, waking me up from disturbing dreams of endless staircases heading up to walls of black windows.

"I'm just going to crash at my sister's," I said.

"Do you want to come over tomorrow?" Maria asked me. "Julio is gone and it's just me and Valenti-na."

Tears bit at the back of my eyes and I looked into the wind so I wouldn't cry.

"Thanks guys, but I'm fine."

But I wasn't and everyone knew it.

Though there were moments I was successful. But mostly there were hours of missing him, of touching my lips and holding back tears or screams.

A rage so sharp it turned to grief.

A grief so big it turned to rage.

I slept most nights at Charlotte's house, and she didn't ask too many questions. At least not with her mouth. Her eyes all but screamed her concern.

I stepped out of the BART station closest to her house (because damn Jack and his argument about debt), the wind picking up my hair and pushing it across my face, and I smacked it back, wrenching it all into a tight ponytail that made my eyes water. In my back pocket my phone vibrated, and I couldn't stop the leap of my heart when I pulled it out.

Please, I thought. Please be him.

But it was Charlotte.

"Hey," I said, trying to sound cheerful as I answered.

"Hey, you on your way?" she asked.

"Ten minutes."

"Can you stop at the corner store and grab some tampons?" she asked.

I stopped in my tracks. Tampons. My period.

Shit.

"Abby?"

"Yeah," I said. "I'll grab some. See you soon."

It's nothing, I thought as I walked up the hill toward Charlotte's condo and the corner store at the end of her block. *It's stress. I mean... things have been so stressful. It only makes sense that my period would be a day... no, two days... late.*

"What's wrong with you?" my sister asked two days later as I was flopped across her purple loveseat, staring at the ceiling, trying to make my stomach cramp and my breasts sore. Trying to will my period into coming.

"Do you feel all right?" she asked.

Four days late.

Four. Days.

The pill pretty much made me regular like a clock. Four days late never happened.

And the morning after pill wasn't always effective.

And I almost told her. But again, I didn't want to be this person again. I didn't want to be the one always coming to her for help. Always needing her.

I was tired of being me.

And if I said it out loud, it was real. Like really real.

"Fine," I said. "Just tired. I think I'm going to go home tonight."

"Really?"

"Yeah. Is that okay?" I was snapping at her and I didn't want to. I didn't mean to. But I was out of control of myself.

"Totally fine," she said with all the patience my sister always used with me.

I left her house and took the train back to my neighborhood and immediately walked to the Safeway, where I bought a pregnancy test.

It sat on my counter for two days.

I lay in my bed, remembering the feel of Jack inside of me that night. The incendiary heat. The terrible beauty of being skin to skin with him. Had I done this on purpose in some way, I wondered, curled under my covers with my blankets over my head.

Knowing he was going to kick me out of his life, had I planned this in some passive-aggressive way?

I sobbed once, hard into my hands. The tears like bricks inside my head, refusing to come out.

No, I thought. *Don't be like this.*

You didn't trick him. You didn't try and get pregnant. You just got caught up in that moment.

Both of us did.

I pushed off the blanket, got up, and took the damn pregnancy test.

When the blue cross appeared, I wasn't even surprised. I couldn't even muster up the fear I'd been living with for four days. It was like the blue cross just obliterated that cloud of fear.

This was real.

It was happening.

I couldn't pretend it wasn't.

Three weeks after that weekend with Jack—I was pregnant with his baby.

CHAPTER TWELVE

Abby

BEFORE

IN THE DAYS after that test, the pregnancy was a secret I clutched to my chest. Like some kind of light I had to protect. I knew what my sister would say.

Oh, Abby...

And she would say it in that *tone*. Slightly disapproving. Slightly disappointed. But loving all the same, like she had—in some way—expected something like this from me.

And maybe, just maybe she was surprised that it hadn't happened earlier.

But it couldn't have happened earlier. Because no man ever got to me like Jack had. No one would have made me forget to use a condom. No one would have turned me so inside out with desire and grief and the ghostly start of love, that I would forget to protect myself.

I cried the next few days. In my apartment. On the

BART. In storage closets in the bar where Maria, Sun, and I were working.

I cried because I was so fucking scared.

And so fucking sad.

And… so fucking happy.

Seriously. Happy. Having this baby could not be bigger problem in my life. A bigger mistake. I had no clue what to do.

But this light I clutched to my chest in the darkness of all that—it was a happy light.

It was an excited light. More than I could have anticipated. More than I could have imagined.

I was going to have a baby.

There wasn't a place I could make for Jack in this situation, not with the secrets and lies. But at the same time this light… this light was so fucking beautiful. And I was alone and I was scared and I wanted to share this. And I wanted to share it with Jack. The joy and the fear.

That was normal, right?

So, in bed, propped up on my pillows, a month pregnant, I took a deep breath and did as he asked that morning in his kitchen. I texted Jack:

We need to talk. It's important.

And the second I sent the text I felt better. I felt less alone, like the burden and the guilt and the fear were not solely on my shoulders. And I fell asleep for the first time in a month feeling like things were going to be all right.

THE NEXT MORNING at eight a.m. I leapt from my bed to find nothing from him on my phone. No text. No voice mail. Nothing. I collapsed backward onto my couch, surprised at how upset I was. How betrayed. He'd kicked me out of his house, what did I actually think he was going to do? Rush to my aid, hold my hand?

Yes. A little.

Dumb Abby.

I'd spent the last few weeks believing he, like me, was lying in bed staring at his phone, my number on the screen and his thumb just barely lifted off the side, paused there, stuck in indecision. In that gray place between hope and fear.

I imagined him in that gray space with me.

And this—this crisis—would bring us both out of that gray space. It would bring us back to each other.

But by Friday afternoon, I realized that was just a dream. A fantasy that wasn't going to happen. The truth was, he kicked me out of his house and he didn't look back, and now I was pregnant.

And I was going to figure this out on my own.

I didn't even bother to text him again. I put him out of my head with more success than I'd ever had. I closed off all roads back to him. I put a tourniquet around the bleeding.

And in the quiet and the hush of my apartment in the middle of the night, I put my hands over my stomach.

"All right," I whispered. "What are we going to do?"

It wasn't going to be easy. My job didn't have insurance and Charlotte made me sign up for the ACA, but that didn't cover everything.

The money I had put aside would keep me going for a few months if the whole birth went okay. If not, I'd be burning through my money in no time.

And after that, it wasn't like I could keep working in bars. The hours were ridiculous.

Tomorrow I would go talk to Vanessa in the offices of Elegance Hospitality, and I'd talk to her about that office job she kept trying to give me.

And my sister... I would tell my sister and I wouldn't be alone. And I'd just... fucking do this.

I smiled up at my ceiling. Sure of nothing except for the fact that this was right. This was the thing I was supposed to do.

I rolled over to my side and the tears trickling from my eyes rolled over my lips and they tasted bittersweet.

I woke up late Saturday morning, near noon. The sun slicing across my room, over my bed. I tested myself, pressed on all my fears and all my plans and everything held. Nothing crumbled. My eyes didn't burn. My heart didn't hurt.

Jack was out of my life.

And I was keeping the baby.

I ached, with a kind of distant grief, but it was tempered with hope. A kind of excitement that felt like the sunshine through my window, warming me up in pieces.

In the kitchen I grabbed my phone to call my sister but I had a voice mail message from an unknown number.

Delivered at 4:30 a.m.

Everything about it felt strange. And dread crept up along the edges of my newfound hope.

I pressed play and bit back a sob when Jack's voice came whispering through my phone.

"Abby," he said, his voice cracked and worn. Tired. "I got your message and I'm sorry I didn't call. I'm sorry…" There was a muffled shout on his end of the phone. "I'm sorry for a lot of things, but I'm not sorry for that weekend with you. I'm not sorry for touching you and for holding you. I'm not sorry for dreaming just for a few days that I had a future with a woman like you. I love you, Abby. It doesn't make sense, but it's the realest thing in my life. I love you. And something… something is going down tonight, and if it ends the way I think it's going to, Patty at the club has a package for you. Be safe, Abby. Be happy."

The message ended and my heart in my throat, I stared at my phone like it could tell me more. I listened again, trying to get some kind of proof that disproved this feeling in my gut. That would alleviate this fear rising in my throat.

Jack left a message because he thought he was going to die.

That was obvious, right? Clear to everyone?

He was saying goodbye.

I listened to the message again, and again, trying to convince myself to not be so dramatic, but the feeling only got worse.

Wherever he was at four a.m. Whatever he'd been doing, he believed he only had a few minutes to live. And in those minutes he called me.

To tell me he loved me.

Jesus, I thought. For the first time in years, I fumbled in my bedside table for my inhaler. I took puffs until I could breathe again. Oh my God.

I called the number back but it was dead. An electronic buzzing scraped at my ears.

What was I supposed to do? Who did I call? The cops?

Quickly I turned on the TV, looking for news. I scrolled through Twitter, looking for any mention of murder on the streets of San Francisco.

There was nothing.

Was he still alive?

The image of him dying somewhere, lying on his back, bleeding into asphalt. Hurt. Scared. Crying. Thinking of me.

I sobbed, dropping the phone.

My knees buckled and I fell down on my kitchen floor.

Okay. Okay. Okay. Think. Think.

I reached for my phone, dropping it once with shaking fingers. I scrolled through my texts and found one from Patty. I called her.

"Hello?" Patty answered on the second ring.

"Patty?"

"Who is this?" she asked, immediately panicked because my voice was so fucking freaked out and wild. I was sobbing and couldn't breathe and I tried to calm myself down.

"It's Abby. From Elegance."

"Yeah, honey, what's wrong?"

"I'm looking for Jack."

"I haven't seen him for two days. I haven't seen any of them for two days. Bates and Jack and Sammy, even Lazarus and every other asshole in a suit in this place took off Thursday afternoon, and I haven't seen him since."

"Jack said he left something for me behind the bar."

"Well, I'm heading there now. I'll call you when I get there."

"Okay, thank you."

I hung up and stood in my kitchen, wondering how long it would take her to get back to me because every second was century.

My phone buzzed in my hand and I stopped breathing with the hope that it was a text from Jack. It was just an email, some spam from a dress store I loved, something I should have known by the tone of the beep. But I stared down at my texts and saw the one from Bates.

The one offering me a job.

The one I didn't respond to but I didn't delete either.

Bates.

Bates would know where Jack was. Bates was with Jack.

Texting him had the flavor of a mistake, but the weight of not knowing was too much. And frankly, if something happened, something serious, I had to doubt he'd answer.

But I couldn't stop myself from trying.

I texted:

This is Abby. I'm looking for Jack. I just want to know he's okay.

Immediately the bouncing dots indicating a return text showed up and my brain buzzed with sudden hope. With a wild relief and panic. Within seconds the balloon of his returning text appeared.

Meet me at the club in a half hour.

Is Jack okay? I texted.

There was no response.

I gaped at my phone and then sobbed hard. Once.

I didn't think twice. I called an Uber (sorry Jack), put my shoes on, and headed out to the club. It was Saturday, just after noon, and I was in a pair of baggy yoga pants, a tank top and a cream sweater pulled over it. My hair was pulled back into two braids, coming undone in a halo around my face.

There was no plan in my head, no conversation I could map out. I had my purse, my keys, and my inhaler, and all I needed was to see Jack.

Because he loved me.

I'm not sorry for dreaming just for a few days that I had a future with a woman like you. I love you, Abby. It doesn't make sense but it's the realest thing in my life. I love you.

I mean, I'm not so stupid that I didn't realize he said those things because he'd been scared. Probably thought he was dying.

But the words swung inside me, gaining momentum. Like a kid on a swing set thinking if they pumped hard enough they'd get the swing to go all the way around the posts.

He was scared, sure. Yes. But the feeling was real. I knew that because the feeling was real in me too.

The ride to the Moonlight took roughly seven thousand years. I sat in the back of some stranger's Honda Civic praying, actually praying between puffs from my inhaler. Tasting blood because I was biting my lips.

Just let him be alive. Just let him be alive. Just let him be alive.

There was nothing to wish for after that. No room for any other thought. If he was alive, the rest would take care of itself.

THE DRIVER DROPPED me in front of the club, which in the daylight looked like any other night club during the day.

A little seedy.

A little forgotten.

The front door was locked. So was the side door, so I ran around back to the alley. It had rained at some point while my world was ending, and my feet splashed through puddles. The spray splattering my legs.

The back door was open, and it felt like seven hundred years ago that I'd watched Jack kick out the guy with the horrible shirt. It felt like something that had happened to a different person.

I pulled hard on the heavy door before stepping into the dark back hallway. I ran past the bathroom where I'd caught Jack praying and cleaning off the blood of the man he'd put in the hospital. I ran past the dressing room mirrors where Sun, Maria, and I had argued about how the men running this place were or were not gangsters, where we'd checked our makeup and done our hair before everything fell to shit.

I felt like I ran past every version of the person I'd been. Shedding all of that like a skin.

It was like what Jack had said about himself three years ago, that version of him was a story he'd heard about another person.

Panting, I pulled open the door that read *Private* across the glass and burst into the wide open club.

"Hello!" I cried, my voice echoing through the empty space.

Patty's head poked up from behind the bar. "Hey!" she said. "Where did you come from?"

"Back door was open."

She shook her head, swearing under her breath. "Here," she said as I approached the bar. "Jack left this for you."

She put a heavy manila envelope on the bar and pushed it toward me.

It was money. I knew before opening it. It was a

stack of cash.

"Is he here?" I asked. The money still on the counter. I wasn't going to touch it. I was never going to touch it. That money was covered in blood. Covered in Jack's blood.

Vomit crawled up my throat.

"No fucking clue," she said. "Someone is upstairs though. I've been hearing a lot of noise. And..." she tilted her head to the end of the bar, where a beautiful Chinese woman in a sleek black rain coat sat drinking a cup of coffee.

She turned and looked at us, her smile a fucking blade. Like danger just...sat beside her.

"I'm with Bates," she said quietly.

Patty and I nodded, like that made sense.

I turned to look at the staircase, the black eye of the windows.

"I gave my notice," Patty said. "My advice, if you want it?"

I didn't.

"Don't go up there," Patty said. "Take this stack of money and run far away from this place and Jack Herrara."

"I will. I am," I breathed. Because that was the smart thing to do. The thing I should do. I just had to find out if he was alive first.

"But you're going up those stairs, right?"

I nodded, because I couldn't speak.

Because I was reckless. And not very smart.

And in love.

"Good fucking luck to you," she said and walked away, leaving me to climb those stairs on my own.

Silent, I went up those stairs. I climbed them like air. Like wind. Like I wasn't there. I had no desire to be heard. To be seen. I wanted to make sure he was alive and then get the hell out of this place.

Go back to my plan. The baby and me.

At the same time I wanted to grab Jack, if he was here, pull him out of this world and into mine. Run with him, all the way to Idaho. Where we'd get our feet under us. We'd figure each other out. We'd have a baby.

I put a hand over my mouth, so I wouldn't make a sound.

The door opened when I turned the doorknob and I found myself in another hallway, surprisingly long and very dark. The end of it opened into another room bathed in mellow light. My angle wasn't the best and I couldn't see anyone in that room, but I could hear voices. Low murmurs.

A sudden shout.

I flinched at the noise and reached behind me for the doorknob, unclear on how I'd been so stupid to come up here.

I knew better than this.

"Jesus, Bates!" It was Jack's voice.

Relief made me giddy. Relief made my legs buckle and my heart leap and I put my hand against the wall so I wouldn't fall over.

"Don't do this," Jack said, and in his voice I heard fear. I heard pain.

"It's already done," Bates said. "You do it, or I will."

And suddenly I wasn't just walking down the hallway toward his voice, I was practically running. Silent as I could be, I crept along the wall, staying hidden by the angle of the doorway as best I could.

I pulled my phone out of my purse and dialed 9 and 1, my thumb poised over the second 1 if I needed it.

The closer I got to the door the better I could hear everyone.

"Those are your choices," Bates said.

I leaned forward until I saw Lazarus's office. It looked like any other office, a wide wooden desk, couches along the side, walls full of non-descript artwork and there, in the middle of the room, was a large man I'd never seen.

On his knees.

Was that Lazarus, I wondered? It had to be.

Standing beside him was Jack.

Bates stood in front of them by the desk, his sleeves

rolled up. His knuckles red and bleeding. His pale blond hair falling into his face. Now he looked young. So young. Impossibly young.

"Pay the debt," Bates said to Jack. "And you're free to go."

"My debt isn't to you," Jack said.

"It is now."

"I m supposed to trust you?" Jack whispered.

"Do you have a choice?" Bates asked and Jack was silent, standing there with his shoulders rigid under his jacket.

"Kill him and you're free," Bates said. "All debts paid."

I put my hand over my mouth, trying to hold back my gasping moan. My heart was thundering in my ears and I wondered how no one could hear me. My fear was the loudest thing on the planet.

"Jack," the man on the floor said, his voice garbled. He turned slightly to spit on the floor and I saw his beaten, raw face. "Don't believe him. You can't trust him. Look at what he's doing to me."

"I'm doing this to you," said Bates in a quiet voice, "because you're a piece of shit."

"And what are you?" the beaten man spat. "What gutter did you crawl out of?"

Bates stepped forward and crouched down in the beaten man's face. "All of them. Every gutter. Gutters you've never even heard of. Gutters so dark. So dirty you can't even fathom them."

"This is about those cunts—"

Jack smashed his fist into the man's jaw, knocking him onto the rug. I jerked back into the shadows, tears squeezing out beneath my eyelids.

"Another word about those women and I'll kill you with my bare hands," Jack said in a voice I'd never heard before.

I leaned forward in time to see Bates grab a gun and point it at the man on his knees, but he was looking at Jack.

"Kill him or I will, and then you'll never be free."

Jack raised his arm, and for the first time I saw the gun he was holding and I could tell, I could tell looking at him that the gun was not empty. It had a silencer on the end. Ominous and chilling.

On the floor the beaten man put his hands up, cowering from the rage on Jack's face.

No, I thought, shaking my head in the shadows, sick and crying and biting my lips until they bled. This was not Jack. Not the man I knew.

"Jack," the man cried, reaching for hem of Jack's rain-splattered coat. "I'm begging you. I have children—"

"So did those women, motherfucker," Bates said.

Jack pulled the trigger.

Despite the silencer it was loud. So loud the night ripped open and I might have screamed. I couldn't be sure. All I knew was that Lazarus hit the floor, blood pooling around his broken body. A hole in his forehead.

I tore my eyes away from the horror and found Bates staring right at me. I'd jumped at the gunfire, out of the shadows and into the well-lit doorway.

He saw me.

I didn't give Jack a second glance, because in that heartbeat, that blood-soaked moment when he pulled the trigger, he wasn't my Jack. He wasn't anyone I knew.

My instincts kicked in and I ran.

PART 2

CHAPTER THIRTEEN

Jack

AFTER

I KILLED HIM.

I was a killer, now. I put the bullet through his skull, splattered his brain across the wall.

I *did* that.

And the relief... oh my fucking god... the *relief*.

It was as if I lost my body for a second, I was the same consistency as the pink mist that had billowed out the back of Lazarus's skull.

That, more than pulling trigger, made me a killer. My relief. The hard clench of joy on my soul, like the bite of a dog that would not let go.

Lazarus is dead.

I killed him.

I could have laughed. I could have fucking wept.

All these years doing everything in my power to not become this thing. And yet, here I was. It had been inevitable in a way. My fight against the tide for nothing.

You can't control what won't be controlled.

Marxist Economic Crisis Theory made real.

And I wished I could stay in this place—numb and mist-like. But I became aware of the ringing in my ears and that my hand was numb and slowly—horrifically—piece by piece I returned to my body. I returned to this room.

The smell of blood and gunpowder gagged me.

Bates's face, calm and knowing like all had gone according to plan, enraged me. Filled me with a blood-red wrath.

I pointed the gun at him. Steady. Calm.

An animal. A machine. Nothing human left in me.

That bullet had killed so much.

"That is an option," Bates said. Like killing him was a thing on a menu I could point to.

"Tell me why I shouldn't?"

"Because someone has to clean up the mess Lazarus left behind," Bates said, leaning back against the desk like I wasn't holding a gun on him. Like his life wasn't in the balance.

But this man was completely opaque. Unreadable.

"The women in the container," I said, pushing the images from my mind.

"The cops will investigate."

"We were a part of that," I said. I didn't give a shit

about the cops. Like any other filthy sinner all I cared about was what was left of my soul.

"We didn't know."

"Does that make us less guilty?" I asked and to my shame I really asked him, like the cold man standing in front of me splattered with blood could lead me out of this horror.

Bates shrugged. Indifferent. Though something about it was not convincing.

"I'm not interested in conversations about guilt," he said. "We're all covered in the blood of the innocent. But you, Jack, despite the body at your feet, are not a killer."

Not a killer?

I was a brother once. A son. A student, even, a million years ago. And despite the last two years and the sickening darkness overtaking me, I clung to the idea that I still was a brother. A son. A student.

A good man, worthy of those things, mundane and ordinary and beautiful.

The fucking empty gun I carried like it meant something, like it negated the beatings I gave. The fear I inflicted.

Like I could split hairs over the nature of my soul.

That was over.

I couldn't undo this. I couldn't pretend it never happened. And I couldn't pretend that I didn't do it for my own freedom, not just for the women we saw tonight, dead in that shipping container, starved of oxygen, their goodbye notes to their faraway children scribbled on the backs of far too few food wrappers.

I swallowed down the vomit screaming up my throat.

The air smelled of burnt blood. Of gunpowder and brain, and I threw the gun into the corner of the room.

"What's next?" I asked, staring at Lazarus's body

"You're free," Bates said, circling the desk to sit in the chair behind it. He sat and grimaced as if the chair was all wrong and he stood up, pulled the chair away, and replaced it with another one. A hard one from the corner.

"My father's debts—"

"Don't interest me," Bates said. "They barely interested Lazarus. He enjoyed the process of trying to squeeze the honor out of you."

I had felt that, keenly. My honor so small I forgot where it was. Forgot I ever had it.

"Why?" I asked. "Why let me go?"

He seemed startled at the question. Or as startled as I ever saw him. A brief widening of his eyes. A slight flaring of his nostrils.

"Why does it matter?" he asked.

"Am I just supposed to believe you?" I asked. I was going crazy. That was the only explanation. I was losing my mind.

"Perhaps I wish someone had given me an out when I needed it."

I never considered who Bates might have been before he became this. That there might have been another road for him.

"Don't," he said, lifting a hand. "I am king now. And kings don't need pity."

"Was this your plan all along?" I asked, connecting dots in my memory. Years of his silent and steady presence at Lazarus's side, how he'd made himself indispensable.

"It would seem to me that a man bent on freedom wouldn't ask these questions?" Bates said. "A man bent on freedom would leave. Fast."

"You mean this?" I asked. "That I'm free. My father. My brother—"

"I don't care about your brother."

I stepped back, away from the blood I'd spilled and the brains I'd splattered on the wall.

With that one miniscule effort, the tiny amount of pressure applied to the trigger of that gun, I'd somehow opened my prison bars.

"Be smart," Bates said. "And leave town for a while."

I thought of that dude ranch Abby told me about. The work and purpose she found there.

Work and purpose.

Two things I never thought I'd have again.

I nodded, feeling like my neck was broken.

"And the girl," Bates said.

"What girl?"

"Abby."

"What about her?" I asked, feeling everything in my chest sharpen and push outward, like there was a bomb exploding in slow motion in my heart.

"Get her out of town too."

"Why?" I asked.

"Tell her if she talks—"

"I didn't tell her anything."

"She saw plenty."

"She didn't see anything."

Bates said nothing, but he looked at me with pity. Enough pity that I knew there was something he knew that I didn't.

I charged the desk, pulling him up by the lapels of that suit he wore like a skin.

"What have you done?" I asked, feeling the cold hand of dread on the back of my neck. His silence enraged me.

"What have you done!" I bellowed, yelling so loud my voice burned. I shook him, and his expression did not change. He smiled at me like I was pitiful, and I grabbed from the desk the gun he'd left there.

"She was looking for you," he said. "I just told her where she could find you."

She was looking for me because of that message I left her. That fucking message. I told her I loved her because I thought I was dying.

"What did she see?" I asked, even though I knew. Because the world turned like a screw, I knew what she saw.

"She saw you put that bullet in his head, and then she left."

"You planned that?"

"Of course not—not even I am that good. I took an opportunity. But it doesn't change the fact that she saw and now, I'm afraid, she's a loose end."

"If you hurt her, I will kill you." I put the barrel of the gun under Bates's chin.

"I don't need to hurt her. You did that yourself." He arched an eyebrow at me. For a second I was sure I was going to blow his brains out. I felt it so sharp I could see it, the splatter of his blood across my face. Across the wall. The jerk of the gun in my hand. "You forgot we don't fuck the innocent, because it's not transferable. You will only diminish it. Ruin it. Men like us—"

"I am nothing like you," I spat in his face, jamming the barrel deep into the soft palate of his mouth.

"You can no longer say that, can you?" he asked,

lifting his chin so he could speak, his eyes flickering to the dead body behind me. "As of ten minutes ago, you are just like me. At least to her you are."

The words struck me like bullets, hitting and destroying the places I'd protected in the last two years.

He was right.

I was no different than the men I'd disdained.

And it wasn't him I wanted to kill. It wasn't him I wanted to hurt.

My heart burned in my chest, every pound a scream.

I put the gun under my own chin, the cold barrel pressing up into my throat.

Something registered in his eyes. A fleeting panic, a shock that vanished as soon as it was there.

"You don't want to do that," Bates said.

"I do," I said. "I should have done it two years ago."

"If you die, who will tell your brother he can stop risking his life in those junkyard fights of his? If you do this thing, I will have to bury your body in the same grave as Lazarus. And no one will ever know."

I didn't care. I didn't give a shit about any of that. My brother would survive, and going down in a grave with Lazarus is everything I deserved.

"If you kill yourself I will send Sammy after the girl," he said. "And Sammy will put a bullet in her brain and leave her body for crows. Or you can walk out of here and take care of her yourself."

"I won't kill her."

"As long as she's silent and not in the city, I don't give a shit what happens to her. But without you, she's just another shots girl. Get her and get gone, or you're both dead."

I sagged. Broken by his words. Beaten by exhaustion. I put the gun down and let go of Bates.

I didn't see or expect the left hook he landed across my face, and I staggered back. He charged around the desk toward me while my ears still rung.

The calm, expressionless Bates was gone. Vanished under something cold and vengeful. Something that had been simmering beneath his still and silent exterior.

As bad as Lazarus was, and he was evil, this man was worse.

"Get the fuck out of here before I change my mind and kill you both right fucking now," he said. I blinked. "GO!" he roared.

I needed no other warning. I was out the door and down the steps. I didn't think about my future. My life. My freedom after all these years.

My world shrunk to a tiny pinpoint of light. Everything now was about Abby. About making sure she was okay. About making sure she got out of the city and stayed safe.

At the bar was a woman I'd never seen before, she stood up from her stool as I came down.

"Are you done up there?" she asked, pulling the tie on her raincoat. I nodded, speechless and numb.

"Excellent," she said and climbed the steps to the second floor. I almost warned her but something told me she knew what she was going to find in that office.

On the bar was the manila envelope I'd left for Abby. The money I wanted to give her so she could realize her dreams; that café where everyone gets what they need.

Where Abby, so sweet, so warm and so bright, gets what she needs.

She'd left without it. I gathered the envelope and slipped it into the pocket inside my sweat-soaked and blood-splattered jacket.

That night, before the diner, before going back to my place, she told me her address, and I drove there without thinking.

Her apartment was an old post-war building, with a security door at the front that I couldn't get through. I stood in the drizzle of a late night and looked up at the windows. One apartment was lit up.

I had no idea if it was hers. I fished out my phone and looking up at that window I called her, believing—hoping—the woman who'd rushed to the club after getting that message from me would not, even having seen what she saw, refuse my call.

She would answer just to know if I was all right.

She would answer just to tell me she was never going to see me again.

I prayed because it was second nature to me. Because I spent most of life praying.

Please answer. Please, my sweet girl, please let me tell you you are safe. Let me tell you you don't have to be scared. But you have to leave town.

But the phone went immediately to voice mail.

"This is Abby. Sorry I can't get to the phone. Leave a message, or, better yet, text me."

I closed my eyes at the sound of her voice. The laughter buried in the sharp edge of her tone, like she was asking me to laugh with her because she was so bad at returning calls.

I missed her. I missed her so much.

And she'd texted me. Days ago. And the only reason she'd reach out was if she was pregnant.

But Abby being pregnant wasn't something I could think about right now.

I couldn't let it in. Not even a little. That would break me into pieces.

"Listen," I said. "I know… I know what you saw, but I can explain. And I know how fucking dubious that sounds, but this is real. Everything has changed and I…I want to tell you you're okay. You're safe. You need to call me. Please. I will not hurt you. Call me please."

I hung up, staring up at that window, rain in my eyes.

But she never did.

CHAPTER FOURTEEN

Jack

AFTER

"DO THE THING," Sammy said, over Lamar's bent head.

"I'm not doing the thing," I said, shivering in my overcoat. The wind whistling across the bay was no joke tonight.

We'd dragged Lamar out of his house into the alley, lined on either side with dumpsters. We'd pulled Lamar away from a poker game surrounded by all his friends, all of them carrying guns. Not one single guy at that table, though, lifted a finger for Lamar when we came in.

Sammy and I, we were the Devil's men. Stand up against us and we'd lay you to waste.

"Do the fucking thing," Sammy said. "Lazarus likes it when you do the thing."

I took a deep breath and turned toward Sammy and Lamar.

Sammy giggled, the giggle of the not totally sane.

"Listen, Lamar… can I call you Lamar?" I asked.

Lamar's mouth was such a mess I couldn't understand what he was saying. *Go fuck yourself,* was the best guess.

I paced in front of him, my boots kicking through the shallow puddles of moonlit rain and the various darker splatters of Lamar's blood.

"Great, Lamar. The problem you're running into here is your business model. You have made the mistake of selling an inferior product in the same market as my boss, for a lower price point. In a free capitalist society this might pull the price down of our product in an effort to regain our market share. But this isn't a free capitalist society, is it, Lamar?"

His response this time was a very clear: *Fuck my mother.*

"Not really an option for you, she's dead," I said, with relief. *If she knew what I'd become…*

"But what we have in this market is a command economic system with one person controlling price, distribution, supply, and manufacturing. And you know who that command is, right?"

Lamar was disturbingly quiet.

"He knows," Sammy jeered. "Everybody fucking knows, Lazarus runs this block, and the next block and the next one."

Sammy was eager to get on with the beating he was supposed to give Lamar in an effort to teach the rest of the entrepreneurial drug dealers trying to make a living in the Loin, a lesson.

"If you tried to sell your shit literally a half a mile to the east or north, we wouldn't have to do this," I told Lamar, nearly pleading with him. "You wouldn't make as much, not at first, but if you kept the price low, word would get out and in time, the market would come to you."

It was suddenly a tragedy that Lamar was so greedy. So stupid. That he was weak this way.

Like my father. Just like my fucking father.

"He's not your father." Abby walked out of the shadows near the entrance to the alley. The streetlights turning her sequined dress to gold.

"I know," I said.

"Jack?"

Lamar wasn't Lamar anymore. It was my father on his knees in front of me, held in Sammy's demented grip.

"Stop," I said. "This isn't real."

"Please," my father begged, his face so broken I could barely recognize him. "I have kids. Two boys—"

"Stop!"

"I'll get you the money."

"Stop!" I screamed but my father wouldn't shut up.

"I'm sorry," he sobbed. "I'm sorry. I'm so sorry."

I punched him, breaking his nose. Red blood splattered across the front of my shirt. I punched my father while Sammy held him and Abby watched and I thought of my brother. Of my mother and the tears she wept.

And how my father's apologies never fixed anything.

I WOKE UP with a start and hit my head against the car's window. Jesus.

It had been a dream. I was in my car, not an alley off Taylor Street. My dad… Abby. I groaned and rubbed my face, trying to shake off the lingering horror and guilt from that shitty dream. My apologies, when I finally found Abby, would mean about as much as my father's did. Which was nothing.

I checked my watch in the gloom of a San Francisco dawn.

Five a.m.

I'd been asleep for a half hour. Shit. I looked across the street at Abby's apartment, the doors still shut, the foyer light in the old walkup gleaming gold.

While I watched, an old woman, a plastic hair protector tied under chin, struggled through the second door into the foyer. My chance.

I got out of my car, ran across the street, catching the outside door just as she was struggling to open it and pull her grocery roller cart behind her.

"Here, let me help you," I said with rusty charm.

"Thank you," she said and trundled past me.

Once inside and past the security code that had kept me in the car all night, I pressed on the button beneath her mailbox, and then touched the cream paper card with her handwriting on it.

Abby Blakely. Unit 212.

There was no answer as I pushed and another person came out, a woman about to go for a run. She gave me some side eye and I tried to smile at her, knowing how bad I looked.

"You're looking for Abby?" she asked.

"Yeah."

"She moved out."

"What?"

"Yeah. Last night. Packed up and left in the middle of the night. Gave me her plants and the shit out of her fridge."

"Do you know where she went?"

The jogger shook her head, even though she clearly knew, and I had the sense refined in me in the last two years that if I pushed, if I pressed, she'd tell me everything.

"She must have gone to her sister's," I said, looking back at her mailbox, like there was an answer in there.

"Probably," she said, but that was all. And it was fine, I could find Abby's twin. I still had people in my

life who could do some shady shit. Finding Charlotte
Blakely in the city of San Francisco wasn't going to be
so hard.

IT TOOK TWO months.

The information came in pieces from a guy I'd
done some work with over the years, a computer
hacker who called himself Domino.

And even he was surprised at how well Abby and
her sister covered their tracks. Which only seemed to
scream to me how desperate Abby was. How scared
she probably still was. That she felt she had to disap-
pear so completely.

Abby broke her lease the first night and emptied
her bank accounts the second night.

Her sister sold her condo.

And they had been living, for a while, in a shitty
hotel out by the airport while waiting for the sale of the
condo to go through. I could only guess from everything Abby had told me about her sister that Charlotte
sold her condo and gave Abby some of the money.

It shouldn't matter. I shouldn't feel anything about
the fact that she took her sister's money, but left mine
on that bar. I understood—I did. But it still stung.

And then Abby left. She bought a shitbag truck and
left town. Drove onto the interstate, and Domino lost

all signal from her. She was living on cash and a new I.D.

But her sister stayed. Her credit card pinged every once in a while. Mostly at a gas station and a grocery store near the airport.

And I spent weeks searching every apartment building in South San Fransisco, leaning hard on every connection I had in that neighborhood, small-time drug dealers and professional gamblers, hookers, and pimps. I combed that neighborhood, staying as low as I could to the ground. Living off money I'd put away in different accounts for my brother if something ever happened to me. Looking over my shoulder every minute of every day.

And now here I was, somehow in front of my brother's apartment. Fucking Shady Oaks. It was so perfect I couldn't believe I hadn't thought of it first. The rent was cheap, there were always rooms, and it was right across from Jim's Diner. Abby had stood next to me that night and read the wrought iron scroll work on the sign.

It would have seemed familiar to her, maybe? She might have picked it not remembering the connection to me, but feeling like she'd seen it someplace before.

And my brother picked it because of our mother and the damn diner.

And maybe after months of searching, this was the

goddamn universe giving me a break. The coincidence of it was enough to break my heart.

My brother and Abby's sister in the same fucking place.

I lifted my hand to knock on the door—the A in the 1A had swung loose from the top and hung upside down—but stopped. Suddenly nervous. Suddenly reluctant.

My brother. My brother was behind this door. It had been two years. Since I went to work for Lazarus, since I said the things I'd said and done the things I'd done to try and keep him safe.

And now here I was, asking for help. For favors.

This wasn't going to go well. Jesse was pissed at me, and had every right to be. And if I told him that he could stop the fights—he'd know why. That the debts were all paid. And I'd paid them in blood.

But I'd come too far and there was too much at stake to stop now, just because it required me to come face to face with my little brother.

Do it, asshole, I told myself.

But still somehow it was harder than it should have been. Because we used to be friends, and I'd broken that as much as I could. Smashed it until it was hate and anger and fear.

We'd had this sleeping bag for those bus rides during high school wrestling season. It was some old thing of Dad's, flannel on the inside, soft from use. Red and slick on the outside, mended by Mom where it had been torn. And we'd unzip the sleeping bag so we could each have the flannel side, and we'd brace our knees against the seat in front of us. And each of us would look out the window at the world waking up as we drove to some meet down the coast.

And the silence we shared—that was as close to a person as I'd ever been in my life until Abby.

Both of them, Abby and Jesse—all I wanted to do was keep them safe. But the dogs were at my door, nipping constantly at my heels. Bates was having me followed and it was only a matter of time before someone found out where I lived.

I had no more choices and there were no more chances to do this the right way. I had now and nothing else.

Jesse's crap lock popped open in no time and I let myself into his rat trap one-bedroom apartment. I tried to feel nothing, I tried to stand there and feel absolutely nothing, but my baby brother was living like a hermit. Like a hermit in a shit apartment, with sheets taped to the windows and cracks in the plaster.

I saw pieces of him everywhere. The old bean bag chair from the house we grew up in. The Iowa State poster tacked over the worst of the wall.

And I also saw what he was doing in a way. The

way he was living so lean, because he imagined I was living so lean. Each of us paying debts we couldn't fucking afford.

And it was my fault.

I should have told him, right at the beginning. Right after the funeral. I should have let him in. Just like I should have let Abby in.

Going it alone had done what for me, exactly? Only made me more alone.

I sat down on the couch and ran my hands over my face. It had been a long two months after two even longer years, and I felt stretched so thin I was see-through.

I'm sorry, Jesse, I thought. *I'm sorry it all got so bad.*

He was in his bedroom. I heard the creak of his mattress and then after a few minutes the sound of his feet hitting the floor, and I braced myself for seeing him again.

But it did little good.

He came out of the bedroom into his living room like a beast. A wolf. He was a predator, heavily muscled. Alarmingly strong. A total stranger.

He'd had a fight two nights ago, that's what I heard from the people who kept tabs on him for me. Reporting the news of these fights like Jesse was an Olympic prizefighter.

The fight had left its marks all over his body. His

face was a black-and-blue mess. His eye swollen. His hands…

His hands looked like my hands the night after going on a run with Sammy. His hands looked violent and terrifying and I couldn't believe we both ended up with hands like that.

"Well, look who finally decided to get out of bed!" I tried for a joke because otherwise I might cry.

He jumped and yelled and fell backward into his door and for a moment, I could have smiled.

"Sorry," I said, still on the couch, unable to get to my feet, because the sight of Jesse after all this time had taken away my strength.

And then, for a second, split second so fast it was like I was imagining it out of thin air—my brother smiled. He smiled like he was happy to see me, and my heart lifted right into my throat.

But then the smile was gone and he was scowling at me hard.

"Jesus," he muttered, "how the fuck did you get in?"

It was exactly what I deserved, so I put aside my hurt and got to my feet. Jesse, the muscle-bound beast, the basement prizefighter, stepped back like he was scared and I had to look away.

I never wanted to be this man. I wanted to be a fucking economist!

"How do you think?" I asked. Breaking into things had been one of my early skills, like numbers. I'd gotten us into more locked swimming pools and arcades as kids than I cared to admit.

"Don't," he said.

"Don't what?"

"Look at me like you miss me."

I missed him like I missed my parents. Like I missed the life I was supposed to have. But two years ago I walked away from Jesse, and when he tried to follow I shut the door in his face.

So maybe he was right. I didn't get to miss him.

I wanted to ask if he remembered when Dad died. How the two of us stood alone—no family, no friends—as they lowered the old man into the grave. On the far edge of the cemetery had been Bates and Sammy, smoking cigarettes and watching us. Like vultures, waiting for our weakness to be revealed so they could gobble us up.

Don't show them anything, I'd said in his ear. *Not now. Not ever.*

We'd both gotten real good at not showing anyone anything. And suddenly, exhausted from the last two months, plagued by nightmare and fear, I wished I never said that. I wished somehow that I'd found a way to really let Jesse be free.

Because this shit he was doing. This was no better

life than mine.

"I heard about the fight," I said.

"You heard I won, then?" he said, all cocky.

"Yeah," I said, trying not to get angry. Because I could see that he expected that. My brother wanted me to be angry. Because anger was easy. "I heard you won. And next week you're going up against Martinez?"

He shrugged, like it meant nothing.

"Out of all the things you could do with your life. You pick this?" I asked, falling into the role even as I tried to stop.

"This is making me a lot of money."

"Yeah," I scoffed, looking around his place. "I can tell."

"I'm good," he said. "I'm really fucking good."

I looked him over, every hard inch of him. He was a machine. All the boyhood beaten out of him.

"Of course you are," I said, feeling like our mother. "But going up against these guys, you're gonna get killed. Or hurt for real. Remember Lars?"

"Of course I remember Lars."

He'd been a neighbor on Burl. A grown-up man living in his parents' basement, playing video games with us because of something that happened to him in the war.

"Yeah, well, you're probably one concussion away from Lars. Tell me, what was the point of getting you free of all Dad's shit if you're only going to get yourself killed in some junkyard fight in a basement?"

"It's not like that."

"Oh, it's exactly like that."

"Well, it's none of your fucking business."

"You could have been anything—"

He went to the door, ignoring the chain I'd cut through. His lock I'd busted; he'd fix it all later.

"Don't rewrite the past, Jack," he said. "You were the one with the future, and you made your choices. I was born to be exactly this and we both know it. You should go. I'm sure you've got important shit to do."

"You kicking me out?" I asked.

He shrugged.

This wasn't why I came here, to fight over ancient history. "I have another question."

"I'm about done answering them."

"Anyone new move in here lately? A girl?"

"Why?"

"Why do you think?"

"Shady Oaks is a long way to go for pussy."

"It's not…it's not like that. I'm looking for a girl. A woman. The woman I want split. I don't know where, I'm pretty sure why, and I just… I need to find her."

"And you think she's here?"

"No, but I think her sister is here."

"Why?" he asked.

"I know they were staying in a hotel out by the airport up until a few weeks ago. I know the sister sold her condo and gave the cash to Abby. I know Abby paid cash for a shitbox pick-up and left town. But the sister... she stayed. And since she didn't have a lot of cash left, she needed a place with cheap rent."

"And you think it's here?"

"Lotta people hide out here." I gave him a pointed look, because what was he doing if not hiding out here.

"I don't pay a whole lot of attention," he said. "People move in and out of this place all the time."

"Yeah. Well, if you see anyone new or hear about some kind of artist—"

"Artist?" he interrupted, sharp and fast, and I turned on him. He was hiding something. I was his brother, I knew him like the back of my hand, and he was lying.

"You heard something?" I asked.

"No, I'm just... What kind of artist would move here?"

"One trying to hide." I stepped toward him, my jacket opening, and I saw him see my gun. And I wanted to tell him about twenty different things. About how it was an old habit. Empty, even. But his face shuttered up hard and he looked away and I stood there and took in my brother's face. Old scars. New wounds.

I barely recognized him anymore. Just as, I'm sure, he didn't recognize me either.

"You don't have to do this," I breathed. "I can give you enough money—"

"What about Dad's debt?" he asked. "How are you going to give me money when we're supposed to be taking care of the money he owes to Lazarus? Last week I made back a chunk of it, you can take it to him. It's not all of it, but it's some."

His eagerness was killing me. His eagerness was all the brother I recognized and loved.

"Stop, Jesse," I said, braving to put my hand on his shoulder. "Dad's debt's been paid."

"How—" He swallowed the rest of the question, because he knew.

The answer was in the tattoos on my arms and the gun under my jacket and the distance I'd put between us. And he couldn't see it, but it was all over my hands. I ran with blood.

And there, right in front of my eyes, I watched my brother's heart break. And I couldn't do this to him—to us—anymore.

"Listen, you hear of a girl moving in, you let me know," I said. "It's important. Real… important."

CHAPTER FIFTEEN

Jack

AFTER

A WEEK PASSED and it seemed all the trails had grown cold. In the cold mist of a dark noon, I went back to my apartment, bringing home Chinese food I wasn't going to eat, because I wasn't eating anything. But the Chinese food—the spicy eggplant and beef with broccoli—it reminded me of her. And that was enough for me in these thin days of looking for her.

I unlocked all my locks, stepped inside my dark kitchen, my body so heavy I was surprised I could move. I closed the door behind me and immediately knew I wasn't alone.

Someone had broken into my house. I gave myself a moment of foolish hope that it was Abby. I imagined her in my bed, the pale warmth of her body such a contrast to the cool of my sheets.

But the person in my house was not Abby. It wasn't my brother or anyone else who might wish me no ill will.

The person in my house was here to kill me. I could smell it in the air.

Feel it in the hair along my spine.

I set the Chinese takeout onto the island and reached into my coat pocket. Every sense alive to the man creeping through the shadows into the doorway to my left.

"Don't go reaching for that empty gun," Sammy said and flipped on the light.

He stood in my doorway in his slick suit and his black leather gloves. Those black leather gloves meant business. They were his *I'm here for blood* gloves.

I shook out of my coat. If this was going to be a fight, I'd need some range of motion.

If this was going to be a fight, one of us was going to need a body bag.

"Hungry?" I asked, still pretending nonchalance. The fact that my old partner hadn't shot me told me he wasn't planning on it. At least not right away. "I've got enough here for two."

"I hate Chinese food," Sammy said.

"I'm not a fan either," I said, looking down at what I ordered. "How did you get in?"

"No one is as safe as they think they are, you know that," Sammy said, with that elegant tilt of his head.

I smiled at him, because I didn't like the guy, but I

knew him and in my cold, sterile life that passed for a relationship. "We doing this?" I asked.

"I'm supposed to fuck you up and get you out of town."

"And?"

"If you don't want to leave I'm supposed to kill you and then go find that girl of yours."

"So?"

He shrugged, that thin shoulder of his belying all of his strength and danger. "I'm not in the mood."

I laughed because the day Sammy wasn't in the mood for blood was a rare day.

He lifted one gloved finger, the leather creaking. The last ones had been ruined with Lamar. I hated that I knew that. "Bates does not find this funny."

"Bates," I said. "How is that going?"

"Fucker is scarier than Lazarus, that's for sure. But…" Sammy shrugged and left it at that.

Serving one despot was just like serving another.

"What's my time frame?" I asked.

"You gotta be gone tomorrow. And I mean it man, you stick around and I get in heat for it, I'm coming back without a warning. I like you and that's the only reason you're not bleeding out your face right now. But you don't listen and I'll do you like you did Lazarus. And then I'll have to go after the girl. Or it will be me Bates is after."

I swallowed, gorge rising in my throat. "Tomorrow?"

"Tomorrow."

I watched him walk out the door, just in case he felt compelled to show me how serious he was. I needed no such demonstration. If I was here tomorrow, I was dead.

And so was Abby,

Sammy left and I grabbed that spicy eggplant and heaved it, needing something to explode in this world. Something to *happen*. Sauce and eggplant splattering against my wall like my brains would.

I left the Chinese food slipping onto the floor, gathered what little of my shit mattered, and went back to Shady Oaks because it was the best lead I had. My brother and my ability to know when he was hiding something the most concrete clue I had in my search for Abby.

Crossing the open courtyard, I ignored the people sitting in lawn chairs around the empty pool like it was summer at the beach, instead of September in some shitty apartment complex in South San Francisco.

When we were kids, there'd been a time when I could intimidate my brother into doing anything. All my chores, sneak me Dad's beer, carry notes to my girlfriends. Anything. But those days ended a long time ago and if he was somehow protecting Abby's sister—

this could get bad.

But beneath the staircase, the apartment next to Jesse's opened up and a woman walked out. White blond hair in wild curls pulled up onto her head. Red glasses.

I stopped, stepped sideways into a slice of shadow left on the ground.

I couldn't get much of a look at her past the hair and the glasses, but every part of my body told me that was her.

That woman, head down, chin tucked into the sparkly scarf around her neck, was Abby's sister.

My fucking brother was living next door to her this whole goddamned time. I watched her leave, walking past the swimming pool sitters with a small wave and a smaller smile until she was out on the sidewalk, walking left out of sight.

And then I broke into her apartment.

I had to give Abby's sister credit—she'd tried with this crappy little apartment. The bumblebee curtains were a nice touch, and the bright red kitchen. I wanted to see Abby in this, in these touches. But I wanted to see Abby in everything. My whole life had narrowed down to seeing Abby again.

Just one more time.

Just once, and then I'd let her go.

Charlotte had a computer set up in the corner,

quite a system, too. Especially considering the shit lock on the door. My fucking brother needed to be taking better care of her, if they were a thing.

Even as I thought that, I knew what I hypocrite I was. Look how good I took care of my girl.

I circled her desk and jiggled the mouse, and on the screen popped a picture of Abby. I was breathless for a moment. I had, over the last too many weeks, told myself that she was not as beautiful as I'd remembered. That there was no way she could be so perfect. But looking at the picture of Abby with her sister, each of them smiling with more joy than I'd felt in my whole life, I knew she was more perfect.

More beautiful. More warm. More real.

I sat down in the chair on the desk and wiggled the mouse again. A password screen came up, and Domino had armed me with all of Charlotte's passwords. For a moment, I felt guilty, but it was a minor guilt compared to my others and I swatted it aside like bug.

The password—*sister212*—was accepted and her landing page opened. She had a ton of files on her desktop. Artwork and research.

I clicked through them as carefully as I could and then—finally – I hit a Facebook messenger window.

She was talking to someone named Cheetara.

Charlotte: *Me too. How are you doing?*

Cheetara: Fine. I took your advice and made a doctor's appointment. I can't keep pretending this isn't happening to me.

Charlotte: Good for you. Are you going to tell him?

Cheetara: No. He can never know. Not ever.

Charlotte: Is he really that bad?

Cheetara: He's bad enough that I'm halfway across the country with all your money just to get away from him.

Charlotte: Did he hurt you?

Cheetara: No. He never hurt me. He'd never…do that. But Char, he hurts other people.

Charlotte: Sometimes things aren't always what they seem.

Cheetara: I saw him kill someone.

I stopped there and stared up at the ceiling for a minute. Jesus, did these two WANT to get hurt? Did they WANT to be found? Wasn't it basic common knowledge that you didn't discuss murder on fucking Facebook?

And why was Abby going to the doctor?

Though I knew the answer to that question, down deep in my gut where I couldn't look at it. Where I didn't want to look at it.

Abby was pregnant. It was real. She was pregnant with my baby.

The need to find her grew to something out of

control. A fire burning through me.

I had to find out where she was. I had to tell her she was safe. That she didn't need to be scared. That she didn't need to worry about me ripping her life apart again.

I needed to give her the money and make sure she was as safe as I could possibly make her.

Her and the baby.

Finally, a few blue bubbles down the list I hit pay dirt:

> **Charlotte:** *How is the job?*
>
> **Cheetara:** *Good. I'm a little surprised how much I like it here.*
>
> **Charlotte:** *Surprised? How about shocked? How about I don't even know you? You went right back to the scene of the worst family vacation in history.*
>
> **Cheetara:** *You have no idea how good the air tastes here.*
>
> **Charlotte:** *Like horseshit?*
>
> **Cheetara:** *I didn't think I'd stay here. I thought I'd stop, look around and move on. But that Help Wanted sign was up in café and it just…seemed right.*
>
> **Charlotte:** *I have a hard time picturing you in a small town.*
>
> **Cheetara:** *You and me both. But It's a relief. He'll never find me here and the cowboys that come into the café aren't half-bad.*

I stood, picked up the monitor, and smashed it onto the floor, knocking over a bunch of other shit in the process, and the violence sent a thrill through me. Wild and familiar. Something I never thought I'd miss, but there it was.

Everything needed to be destroyed. Her entire Facebook account needed to be scrubbed, because if I found her, so could Bates.

After smashing it all I left Charlotte's apartment, turned toward Jesse's to tell him to get Charlotte out of town and if he couldn't do it, I would—and caught him just as he was about to leave.

He got one look at me and could not hide the fear. Or the guilt. But mostly fear.

And I swallowed down my regret over that.

I couldn't see the girl, but the way my brother's eyes kept glancing behind the door it was painfully obvious she was standing right there.

Just as it was obvious my brother would kill me before he let me hurt her.

Abby's sister.

There was kind of a directionless jealousy I felt, for my brother to have the object of his affections so close, for Charlotte who still had such a connection to her sister. For myself because my brother once felt that kind of protection toward me and clearly didn't anymore.

And I had no one to blame but myself for all of it.

I couldn't name it, this pang of grief and happiness. But it was so painful it tied like a knot in my chest.

"Going somewhere?" I asked.

"What do you want?" Jesse demanded, and I wanted to shout that I didn't have time for this bullshit. He glanced behind the door and my anger at him, at everyone standing in my way, raged out of control.

"You know what I want. I want your neighbor. The blonde with the tits." I was being an asshole, crude on purpose, putting everyone on edge because I felt like my skin was on fire. I tried to step inside the apartment but he got in my way, not letting me in.

"It's like that, is it?" I asked.

"It's like that."

Fine, I thought. *Then it's like this*, and I pulled a gun from the pocket of my long overcoat.

"It's still like that," he said.

I turned the gun so it was facing the door, the barrel pointed right at where I imagined Charlotte's head might be. Or at least close enough to let Jesse know I was serious.

"It doesn't have to happen like this," I said. "Just let me in."

"You hurt her and I will kill you."

I smiled at his dramatics and then nodded. "I am duly warned."

He stepped back. Proving once again my theory that an empty gun was just as effective as a loaded gun, ninety-nine percent of the time.

I closed the door behind me and got my first good look at Abby's sister. This was not the way I'd ever imagined this happening, but it was in the end exactly what I deserved.

And despite the shattering pain of that, I couldn't help but smile. I could see Abby in her, yes. So much. But I could see all the ways Abby loved her too. The way she stood there with chin up but her eyes so terrified, wearing bright red glasses and a *This Pussy Grabs Back* tee shirt.

"Charlotte," I said, feeling awful about the computer I just smashed. She saved everything on the cloud, Domino had found out that much, so it wasn't all gone. "You are just as your sister described you."

Charlotte looked at the gun in my hand and sneered. "And you're just as she described you. A dangerous sociopath."

Sociopath. Oh, how I wished that were true. Perhaps that would help all of this make sense. But instead I was just a man, doing the best he could, making mistake after mistake.

Smoothly, my brother got between us. I wanted to tell him he shouldn't worry about me hurting her. But what was the point? I was so damn tired. I put the gun back in my pocket. An empty prop that served its purpose.

"It looks like we've fallen in love with sisters. It's so ironic, isn't it? I mean the odds have to be… what, one in seven million?" I asked my brother.

"My sister doesn't love you," Charlotte said. "She ran away from you because she's scared of you."

"I know," I said. "I know. I wanted… I wanted to protect her from that part of my life."

"You did a shit job of that."

"Maybe," Jesse muttered over his shoulder, "don't provoke the guy with the gun?"

I pulled the gun back out of my pocket and took the clip out of it and showed it to them.

"Empty," Jesse said, surprised.

"Yeah," I breathed and threw the gun and the empty clip on the table. "I've been carrying that fucking thing around for two years, most of the time without any bullets. Praying I didn't have to use it."

"That," Charlotte breathed, "sounds awful."

"Not as awful as actually using it," I said quietly, staring down at my hands before looking up at Jesse. "I'm out," I said. "Out of the life. I'm leaving tonight. Debts are paid. I'm done."

"You're leaving San Francisco?" Jesse asked.

"I'm going to find Abby," I said.

"You won't," Charlotte said.

"I have a pretty good idea where she is," I said. "She told me about that vacation your family took when you were fifteen. The ranch and the small town."

I read a whole bunch of reactions to that across Charlotte's face, all of them shocked and worried, and then she pulled all of those feelings behind a haughty, angry mask that was so much her sister I felt smacked.

"Well, if you do find her, she won't have anything to do with you. At all," she said.

My chest lifted with a soundless laugh. "That is much more likely. Why does she need the doctor?" I asked, the question burning in the darkness of my heart exploding into the air. "Is she all right?"

"I'm not telling you shit," Charlotte said and I expected nothing less.

"I will find out for myself soon enough," I said, sounding ominous as hell, and I wanted to tell their terrified faces that I meant Abby no harm. That I would die to protect her from the mess I made, but there was no point. And worse, there was no time.

I wondered, briefly, if this was the last time I would see Jesse. And I found I couldn't help myself from being his big brother just one more time. I took a deep breath and looked him in the eye, willing him after all these years to feel what we used to have. To trust me like he used to trust me.

"Tell her. Tell her everything," I said. "If you want a

shot with her, you've got to tell her. And if she stays after that... don't let her go." I then turned to Charlotte. "I'm sorry this is how we've met. I hope... well, let's just say I hope a lot of things."

My words dried up and my time was gone and my very last chance was slipping right out of my hands, so I just nodded in the end and gave Jesse one last look. Soaking in the man he'd become and glad, at least, that I'd protected him in the small way that I could

My best was a shabby thing, tattered and small, but I'd done it for him. Given it to him. And it was all I'd had.

"Bye Jack," Jesse murmured and I walked out the door.

Abby, I thought, now, it was only Abby.

CHAPTER SIXTEEN

Abby

AFTER

"More coffee?" I asked, taking the pot over to Dale and Doug Hardt. I didn't really need to ask; they would drink coffee until the café ran out of the stuff.

Every few days when they came in and I served them cup after cup of coffee, they reminded me of Jack's mother in a diner with her two kids, the endless cups of coffee making her happy.

I shook the thought away, like I'd been shaking away every thought of Jack. It was as if every few minutes I'd pull myself out of the creek of some memory covered in leeches. And I had to pluck them off one by one or risk losing all my blood.

Dramatic, yes, but I was in fucking small-town Idaho, pregnant with a killer's baby and living above the café where I worked.

These were dramatic days.

Oddly, they were good days too. Quiet. Full of

work I liked. Full of people that didn't ask more from me than what I could give.

Idaho had been a good choice. The right choice.

"Thank you," Dale said—or was it Doug, really hard to tell them apart. They wore the same tan Carhartt jackets and the same denim pants. Fluorescent orange hunter caps on their balding heads.

I loved these twin men in their sixties, who had a small cattle farm outside of town. They were practically the opposite of my sister and I in every way, but just the way they ate together, and handed each other the things they needed before they could ask, reminded me so sharply of Charlotte I wanted to cry.

"You want the special?" I asked. The special was always a hot turkey plate, and they never ordered anything else. I liked that about them too. Reminded me of sushi with Charlotte and extra California rolls.

"Not today," Doug said.

"Thought we'd try one of them muffins," Dale said, pointing to the pastry case I'd put together. It was nothing special, all muffins and cookies I'd bought from the store, but the little elevated pastry case made it seem special. And it had worked. People were buying the muffins and the cookies, coming in at three o'clock for extra cups of coffee and something sweet.

Yeah, I know, it was ridiculous to be so proud of such a thing, but Margaret the owner treated me like

I'd just created a new business model. And the praise was balm on my ragged soul.

I lifted my eyebrows in surprise and smiled at them. "Look at you two, branching out."

Doug—or was it Dale—blushed, but only at the tips of his ears, and I went to get them the muffins.

My body felt different this month, all over bigger, not just at my stomach, which was just now beginning to swell. I covered it up with the apron I wore, and my looser shirts, but even if people couldn't see how I'd changed, I could feel it. My breasts were bigger. My thighs. My hands and fingers felt twice their thickness, and my feet too.

Some days I woke up and felt like a new puppy with paws the size of dinner plates.

The bell over the door rang as someone new came in and I cried out "Go ahead and sit anywhere, I'll be with you in a second."

The café had six booths and a tiny eat-in counter, and in the afternoons it was only ever the Hardt twins and a few high schoolers coming in after school for big plates of French fries.

I put two muffins on plates and turned back to the front of the café, where the guys sat in the window seat next to the door.

The door where a man stood in a long overcoat. His black curls a mess around his weary face. His midnight blue eyes pinning me to the wall with a fever-bright intensity.

Jack.

For a moment, honest and blazing, I was so happy to see him. So *relieved.*

He's here.

And then the fear set in and the plates fell from my numb fingers to shatter onto the floor and I jerked back hard into a table, nearly falling over.

Jack reached for me, and the Hardt brothers were up and out of their seats, and I put my hands up and shouted: "No!"

All three men stilled. Looking at each other and then at me.

"You all right up there?" asked Margaret from the back where she was sitting on her stool in the corner of the kitchen, reading a newspaper, waiting for an order to come in.

"I'm fine," I cried over my shoulder. But my hands were still up like I had any hope in warding him away.

"Abigail," Doug said. I knew it was Doug because he called me Abigail. I'd talked him down from Ms. Abigail, because when he called me that for the first few weeks I'd felt like a Sunday school teacher.

"You okay?" Doug asked.

No. No I wasn't okay. I shook my head.

"Is this man a problem?" Dale asked.

"Yes," I said, and just like that Dale and Doug turned to face Jack, a solid wall of Idaho stubbornness between me and my baby's father.

But then I remembered that gun. The trigger pulled by this man's finger, and I could not believe I put these men at risk. "No!" I said just as quickly. "No, boys, he's... he's an old friend. I just... I got startled for a moment."

"You don't seem startled," Doug said. "You seem scared."

I was. I was terrified.

He found me. That seemed ominous. Everything about him seemed ominous. The overcoat, the exhausted lines around his eyes, the stern set of his mouth like he'd been sent to do an impossible and distasteful job.

Like kill me.

"I mean her no harm," Jack said, lifting his hands as if to show the guys he had no weapons, but I was looking at that overcoat, remembering what this man kept in his pockets.

"She doesn't seem to believe you," Doug said.

"Perhaps you'd best go outside," Dale said.

Jack looked at me over their fluorescent hats like he didn't understand how I'd gotten such a strange pair of bodyguards. But all I could think was I would not have them hurt on my account.

"Thank you, guys." I bent down and grabbed the muffins from the floor and the plates that had broken in half. My hands were shaking; I cut my finger on a broken plate and barely felt it. I felt my heartbeat in my eyeballs. I imagined the baby in my stomach, turning circles without knowing this nightmare.

I forced myself to laugh. To smile even as I turned to face these three men. "Everything is fine, guys. Margaret," I yelled over my shoulder. "I'm taking a break."

The stool where she perched back there creaked, and she shuffled to the doorway between the kitchen and the dining room. "Go on then. I got it."

She was a version of Mrs. Claus with her white bun and her bright cheeks. But she cursed like a sailor and drank from a bottle of hooch she kept over the fryer.

The Hardt brothers watched me with their runny brown eyes, their age-spotted hands clenched into fists that would be ineffectual against Jack's razor-sharp edges.

"It's all right, really," I said, patting their shoulders as I squeezed between them. I tried to smile at them, but it felt like a grimace.

"You stay where we can see you," murmured Dale. "You don't go nowhere with this guy."

"Don't worry,' I said, facing Jack. "I'm not going anywhere with him."

Jack nodded as if he understood my warning and he held open the door for me. I grabbed my sweater from the hook by the door and walked past him, refusing to feel him, or smell him. Denying my body's demands for just one small taste of him, in any way.

My body had no sense when it came to this man. It never had.

Out on the main street, things were quiet. But they usually were in Bloomfield. It was why I liked it. Why I picked it. I felt safe here. I felt completely invisible.

I'd gone to Silver Falls first, but when my sister texted that he was coming for me, I'd run. Found this place. This job. Remarkably like the old place. The old job.

Apparently, I didn't run far enough.

"How did you find me?" I asked when the door shut behind us. I wrapped my sweater closer around my body—not that it was cold, but it made me feel more protected against him. Like my ten-year-old Gap sweater could stop his bullets. Or the brush of his eyes against my skin.

"I went to Silver Falls first," he said. "Followed you from there." He shrugged like it was nothing.

A car drove past, a kid in the passenger seat watching us as he went by.

"What are you going to do?" I asked, my mouth dry. My throat closed. I watched that car until it turned out of sight.

"Can you look at me?" he asked, stepping closer so I felt the heat of him through the weave of that Gap sweater.

I glanced up, all my bravery mustered and at the sight of his weary smile, I looked away. At my feet. The Converse I'd worn the night we met. The never-ending wind blew the pieces of my hair that had fallen out of my braid across my face and I left it, not wanting to see any part of him.

"Just tell me what you're going to do," I whispered. "Are you here to threaten me? Kill me?"

He reached for me, for the bulge of my stomach revealed by the wind blowing my shirt against me, and I flinched away, stumbling backward.

Behind me there was a knock on the glass and I turned to give Doug and Dale my best "it's all right" smile because they'd seen me flinch.

"You're pregnant."

"No," I said and shook my head.

"Abby…I can see you." Again he reached forward like he would touch my stomach, and there was no way that was going to happen.

"Don't," I all but hissed, looking right at him so he could see how serious I was. How much I meant this. He had no right to me anymore. "Touch me."

His face was so thin. So broken. The same but painfully different at the same time. Did he look at me and see the same thing? See all the ways I was different inside my skin?

"You didn't take the money," he said. "At the bar."

"Why would I?"

He gaped at me. "Abby…the baby. Your future—"

I couldn't take it anymore. The not knowing. His weary grin combined with my bloody memories. Daring him really to just get on with the business of silencing me, I put my chin up.

"Do I have one?"

CHAPTER SEVENTEEN

Jack

AFTER

SHE THOUGHT I was here to kill her.

She was pregnant—it was obvious despite her denial. And she still expected me to kill her. That it surprised me was strange. For the last two years of my life, everyone upon whose doorway I landed expected me to kill them. Or hurt them. Intimidate and silence them.

How quickly I'd shed that skin. In searching for her, I'd stopped being anything but this man looking for a woman. Every other part of me shaved off by my efforts.

But here she was, screwing those parts of me back to my body. Reminding me of the monster I'd been.

"I'm here to tell you you're safe," I said, wishing I could be anything but what I was. Wishing I could do anything to take away that look in her eye of fear and distrust. "No one is after you. No one is after your sister."

"I don't believe you," she spat. Her eyes shooting out sparks. She wore no makeup, and her hair was braided in a long tail down her back, and she looked so beautiful it hurt. It squeezed me, her beauty, and I glanced away.

"I'm sorry," I told her, staring into the window of a dress shop across the street with unseeing eyes. "I'm sorry you don't believe me, but it's true."

She laughed, humorless and dry. Wind pushed stray pieces of hair across her face and I jealously watched as she pulled them away from her beautiful eyes.

I want to touch you. I'm so cold and you're so warm and I have no right to ask. No right to even want it. But God, I want to touch you.

"It's funny, isn't it? How relative that is? *True*." She said the word like it tasted funny in her mouth. Like it tasted bad.

"You're having my baby," I said. "That's true, isn't it?"

"I'm having *my* baby," she answered staunchly.

She stared up at the endless pale blue sky and I stared at her—her swollen belly.

My baby. Our baby.

There was a reaction in my body to this news. To this truth. But I couldn't feel it now. Or make sense of it. Or understand it. My goal... my only goal was to make her feel safe.

"Do you believe me? That you're safe? No one—including me, especially me, is going to hurt you."

"It's a little late for that kind of promise isn't it?" she asked, reminding me so clearly of that awful morning when I kicked her out of my condo.

"There are so many things I want to tell you," I said. "So many things I should have told you.

"It's too late," she said. "It's so past too late. You told me the truth, that you were a bad man. I even knew that to be true. But I wanted to believe something else. I wanted to believe the economics student. The little boy at a diner with his mom. The teenager who joined the wrestling team just to spend time with his brother. I chose those things to be true, when I knew better."

"I was those things," I said.

"But you're not anymore, are you?" Now she looked at me, her eyes bullets straight into my chest. "I saw the truth that night."

"I'm out of the organization," I said. "I don't work for Lazarus or Bates anymore."

She laughed, but nothing was funny. "Did you kill Bates too? Is that how—"

I stepped closer because she was talking too loud. She was being too reckless. Her mouth shut fast and I watched her throat bob as she swallowed. She tried to step away but I wouldn't let her. This wasn't a conversation she could run from.

"You're safe," I whispered. "But not if you talk like that. Not if you're reckless, Abby." I begged her to understand that, that this wasn't a goddamned game. "Do you get that?"

Her neck and cheeks red, she nodded and the wind carried her scent to me, coffee and fried potatoes and her, beneath it. Roses and sparkle.

"I didn't kill Bates," I murmured in a low voice that didn't carry past us.

"Is that supposed to change what I saw?" she asked. "Erase it?"

"No, I just hoped it would make you feel more…" I didn't know how to do this. How to make anyone feel comfortable around me. Those three days we spent together had been such an anomaly. I'd put down all my walls. All my armor. "…at ease."

"You told me your fucking gun wasn't loaded," she said with a laugh.

"It wasn't my gun," I said like it mattered. Like those little details meant anything. "Bates knew I didn't carry it loaded. He always knew it." Which made my little protest, my clinging effort to remain at some level the me I needed to be, a joke. A charade.

But I looked at her face, resolute and calm, and I

knew it didn't matter. Not to her. Not anymore.

"I never killed anyone," I said. "Not until that night. And it doesn't change anything. But that is true. And I've wondered over and over again in the last three months if I'd told you why I was the person I was, if it would have mattered. If I'd told you about my father and his debts and what they would have done to my brother, if it would have made this moment not happen."

"Nothing can change what happened, Jack."

"Except you're pregnant," I said. "And that changes everything."

Abby

AFTER

I SWALLOWED BACK my childish denials. Because who was I kidding? I was having Jack's baby. We both knew it.

"You went to the doctor? Is everything okay?" he asked, like he wanted to see an ultrasound.

"How do you know that?" I asked, chill sweeping over my body. "That I went to the doctor."

"Because you were talking about it on Facebook," he said. "That and other things you shouldn't have talked about on Facebook."

Right. The murder.

"Is that how you found me? Facebook?"

"That's part of it, Cheetara."

He was teasing me. Oh, how sweet that was, that he was teasing me over that name, and I suddenly wanted to tell him all about my sister and me playing Thundercats when we were kids. I wanted to make him laugh with the story of how my sister made me a lasso.

But I swallowed all of that. All those words.

"I thought I was being so careful," I said, feeling ridiculous. The Cheetara code name. The fact that I'd tried to keep my secrets to myself in order to not burden my sister any more than I already did, only to fling them out into the world for her to handle. Honestly. If it wasn't so terrifying it would be hilarious.

"Tell me," he said. "Just tell me the truth. Are you healthy? Is the baby healthy?"

"Why do you feel I owe you that? The truth? When you have never given me the same? How is that fair, Jack?"

It was starting to get cold, the wind blowing down the street from the mountains to the east of us. He ran his hand over his face and I stopped myself from telling him he looked tired. I stopped myself from caring that he looked like he might fall over at any moment.

"My father was killed by Lazarus," he said, dropping his hands to stare at me. Right at me too, like I couldn't look away from him and the naked nature of his gaze. This was the man in those nights at his house. This was the man whose skin I knew by heart. It was shocking to see him again.

"I'm sorry," I said.

"Jesse and I were in college. Mom was already dead and they found Dad shot in the back of the head in the passenger seat of his car."

I put my fingers to my lips, holding back my sounds of sympathy.

"Jesse and I came back from school and we were cleaning stuff up. Getting the house ready to sell and all that stuff. Going through pictures. It was... endless, you know," he said. "I just couldn't believe how much stuff my parents had. How many things they'd kept and how far we'd all spun away from each other. Anyway, we were mostly done, Jesse and me were both getting ready to go back to our schools, Jesse really fucking reluctantly, but I didn't want to hear it. I just wanted to get back to classes, finish my degree and put all this shit behind me. No, I needed Jesse to just...go."

"What happened?"

"Bates showed up."

I sucked in a breath of air and then another, forcing myself to breathe.

"My dad owed Lazarus a half a million dollars."

I thought of that tattoo under his arm. *500,000.*

"And we had two weeks to pay it back, or one of us could work it out in trade, or one, perhaps both of us would get shot in the head in the passenger seat of some car. That was the deal Bates presented to me. There was no way we had that kind of money. No way we could get that kind of money. So I sent Jesse back to school, telling him I'd handle it, and I dropped out of school and went to work for Lazarus."

"Oh my god."

"Mostly, I was like a trophy he kept around. A warning to his other associates that debts got paid no matter what. That no one's child or wife was safe."

"What happened to Jesse?" I asked.

"He quit school, came back, tried to pay off the debt by risking his life in those fucking fights. And it didn't matter. I was already in it. I already couldn't get out."

"Didn't he try and stop you?"

"Of course," he said with a wan smile. An exhausted broken smile in his exhausted defeated face.

I don't care, I told myself, curling my hands into fists so I wouldn't reach for him. Push back that tangle of curls over his forehead.

"That night," he said. "The night you saw…what you saw…we'd spent the night before that in Oakland, picking up what we thought was a shipment of drugs. We got the container open and it was…" He looked away, up to the sky as birds flew overhead. "It was women."

I felt myself gag.

"They were all dead."

"Stop," I said and he did. He closed his mouth. Coughed and didn't say any more.

He would keep it inside if that was what I asked for. "Then what?" I asked.

"You saw what happened next."

"No. How did you get to that point? In the office?"

"Lazarus was threatening war on everyone we met. Every dock worker, every security guard. I thought we were all going to be killed. But we got him back to the Moonlight and we all kind of lost our minds. Bates... just started beating Lazarus. Like... I'd never seen him do anything like that before. And then he told me if I killed Lazarus, the debt would be paid. I could go."

"And so you shot him? So you could be free."

"I've been running that night over and over in my brain for months, but I think... I think I shot him because I wanted to. Because he was such a cancer. An evil. And the world was better without him in it. I shot him because in my upside down world, it was the right thing to do. Bates just gave me the excuse."

"But he set you free."

"For the price of Lazarus's life and my silence, yes. He set me free. I have to stay out of the city for a while.

You should too, because of what you saw."

"He texted me," I told him. "He told me to meet you at the Moonlight. That's why I went. I wouldn't have gone, but I was so scared for you. After that message—"

The message when he told me he loved me. Neither of us said a word about that. We stiffened. He coughed. We might never be able to talk about that voice mail. It might just be a thing that happened in the past. Like those three days in his house.

Memories. That's all.

"I think he brought you to the Moonlight," he said, "because he knew I was lying to you and he knew how you felt about me. And he wanted you to see who I really was."

"Why is that any of his business?" I asked.

He shook his head. "I don't understand Bates. I never will."

We stood there for a long time, silent and breathing. The world spinning around us.

"I pushed you away, Abby," he said, "because I never thought I'd be free. I couldn't let you get attached. I couldn't get attached, because I believed I would always be owned by Lazarus."

The door to the café opened and Margaret stuck her Mrs. Claus head out and swore at me.

"The hell you doing, Abby? You got those boys in

there wanting to call in the National Guard."

"Sorry, Margaret," I said. "I'll be in in two seconds. Tell Dale and Doug that I'm fine. That everything is fine."

She muttered something foul under her breath and went back inside.

"That's my truth, Abby," he said. "I've done terrible things, telling myself I was keeping my brother safe. Paying my father's debts. I've turned myself into someone I never dreamed I'd be. And I'm not telling you that to make you sympathetic, but just to make you understand how I didn't, not once, know what to do with you. How to want you and not hurt you. How to let you be in my life in any way. I messed up, I know. But I don't know if I could have done it any differently."

I understood that. I didn't want to, but I did.

"And I know you want me to leave. I understand that. But I can't, princess." The endearment made me flinch. It made me cringe and ache. Because part of me so badly wanted to still be his princess. "You're pregnant. And you're alone."

"Lots of women have babies on their own."

"Not my baby, Abby."

His eyes... oh, his eyes. His eyes told me he wasn't going anywhere. His eyes told me he would not leave, and he would not push me away. Never again.

Something had happened to me since coming out here. I stopped wondering what my sister would do if she were in my place. I stopped wishing I was smarter about some things. Leaving the city and running out here had pulled away some of the doubts I lived with. Largely because there wasn't any time anymore.

That version of me, so beautiful but so insecure—it seemed like a long time ago. A different person, even. I didn't see my beauty when I looked in the mirror anymore, I just saw my face.

I just saw me.

And I looked at Jack and I tried to just see him, but it was difficult because he wasn't easily seen. He was buried deep and down. And out of sight.

But I'd seen him, those three days in his apartment, I wasn't making that up. I'd *seen* him.

And that man, the one I'd seen, he deserved the truth.

"I'm healthy. The baby is healthy."

"Thank you," he whispered, his eyes damp.

"I have to go back to work," I told him and opened the door.

"I'm not leaving," he said. "I'm staying in town until we get some things figured out."

Probably he wanted to talk about the baby and the future and custody and money, and I didn't care about those things.

Well, I did, sure. But mostly… mostly I cared about him.

I ran hundreds of miles, and here I was right back in the same spot.

In trouble. With Jack Herrara.

CHAPTER EIGHTEEN

Jack

AFTER

THE BLUEBIRD MOTEL was nothing special, but despite the crappy mattress and the sound of semis rolling by on the highway outside my door, I slept like I was dead. I woke up disoriented and strange, reaching like I did every morning for my anxiety. Searching through my subconscious for all the things I worried over.

Abby.

The baby.

Her future.

And I realized they were all here, within reach. I'd found her, and she was healthy, and the baby was healthy, and the future was not a cold blank place.

I showered and then, standing in a threadbare Bluebird Motel towel, wiped the steam off the mirror and carefully shaved, putting more into my appearance than I had in years. I got dressed. Having left all my suits behind in the city, I planned to never wear a suit again. Not ever. And instead I wore the clothes of who I'd been. The son, brother and student.

Old faded Levi's and a fisherman's sweater my mother had knit for me before she died. All of it still fit, thanks to the weight I'd lost in the last three months. I was like a razor-sharp version of myself.

And I liked it. I liked the sweater against my skin and I liked the age in my eyes.

I wondered if Abby would like it. If she would see this version of me and miss the gangster in the suits with the scowl.

I liked the version of her I'd seen yesterday. She looked somehow younger, with that braid down her back and no makeup, but also older. More solid. More grounded. And I knew that I had done that to her.

I had taken away some of the brilliance that had attracted me to her. I had wiped away some of the shine.

And I had no business admiring what I'd left behind. No business thinking her more beautiful for the pain I'd caused her.

But I did.

I grabbed my keys from the uneven table beside the door and headed out, planning to go back to the café. I would give her the money she left behind, and I'd try to convince her to let me take care of her in whatever capacity she felt comfortable with.

I expected her to resist. I expected to have to wear her down.

Halfway into town I saw the church spire, and my soul recognized the beacon as something I needed. I hadn't confessed once since the murder. Since Abby. The baby. I'd been clinging to my sins like a rosary.

I turned into town earlier than I would to get to the café. Over the tree line I followed that spire until I was stopped in front of a Catholic church that was sandwiched between a train overpass and the public library.

Without thinking, I put the car in park and went inside. Embraced immediately by the smell of incense and mildew. Wood cleaner.

I loved that a Catholic church in small-town Idaho was in so many ways no different than a Catholic church in San Francisco. The gory stations of the cross plaques. The blood-red stained glass. The crucifix.

The violence of it all made me feel at home.

"Can I help you?" a man asked, poking his head up from behind the lectern at the front of the building.

"I'm, ah, just passing through," I said, walking slowly up the center aisle.

"Well, we're always happy to see those passing through. I'm Father John." The man came down the stairs, wearing the collar of his faith. The black clothing of his calling. "I'm trying to fix a microphone problem at the lectern, but I think I've only made it worse. Betty told me I would make it worse, and now I've only proven her right."

"I'm Jack," I said, feeling tongue tied. I only talked to priests when they were behind screens in confessional. "When are your hours of confession?"

"Sundays," Father John said. "After Mass."

Sunday was four days away. I must have looked crestfallen because he said, "But I have time to talk now, if you'd like."

"Talk?" I asked, like the idea was horrible.

"Not so different from confession, really."

Except that it was completely different than confession. There was a script in confession. There was a screen between me and the priest. This... was not that at all.

He sat down in the pew closest to him. "Please, have a seat." He gestured to the pew in front of him and I found myself sitting down.

"What brings you to Bloomfield?" he asked, his blue eyes piercing beneath bushy white eyebrows.

I killed a man.

That's what I wanted to say, but I wasn't there yet. I might never be there. I might never be able to say those words to a priest in my life.

"A woman."

"Uh oh." He said it with a smile, a tired old joke that had the effect of making me smile.

"She's having my baby." Even saying the words was ridiculous. They sounded outrageous coming out of my mouth. Abby was having my baby.

"Are you married?" He sounded stern and disapproving and I very nearly got up, but I'd come here for this. I'd come to be judged and then forgiven.

"No."

"Are you going to be?"

I hadn't thought of that. Married? It was the twenty-first century, marriage was hardly a requirement for being a family. But… married? The idea of it, the quiet nature of the word and all the strange comfort it would provide. Me and Abby and the baby. Forever.

"If… if that's what she wants."

"What do you want?" he asked, and I turned sharply to look at him.

He held his hands out in front of him. "It seems like a reasonable question. Do you want to marry her?"

Yes, I thought, so small and so quiet. *Of course. She is all I want.*

"I don't think what I want matters," I said.

"Who told you that?" he asked, sounding angry on my behalf.

"It's… well, it's complicated."

He sighed and sat back against his pew. "I think that's bullshit."

I gaped at him in surprise and he smiled at me.

"The important things," he said. "Love. Forgiveness. Commitment. Faith. Hope. They are simple things with yes or no answers. You love or you don't. You believe or you don't. You forgive or you don't."

I sat there for a long time, and he sat with me silently.

"Son," he finally said, "you are welcome here for as long as you like, but I need to fix that microphone before Betty finds out I broke it worse."

"Thank you," I said.

"Remember," he said as he passed, a friendly hand on my shoulder. "There are worse things than love."

Perhaps that was true.

But I couldn't think of them.

I SHOWED UP at the café an hour later, not sure if she would be working but hoping she would be. Because I had real doubts anyone in that place would tell me where she lived.

My plan, such as it was, was to sit there and eat and drink coffee until she came in.

Walking into the coffee-scented air with the bell ringing overhead was such a familiar thing, and so soon after the piercing familiarity of church, I felt overcome in a way. By all the parts of my life. My mother and my past. My brother. And now Abby and perhaps my kid.

Abby was there. Behind the counter. An apron tied around her waist, revealing the small swell of her stomach.

She looked so different than she did in the city. Plainer. Simpler. Fiercer.

I wondered if other people looked at her and just thought she carried some weight there. Or did everyone know she was pregnant?

I wanted—like a caveman—for everyone to know she was pregnant. With my baby.

She glanced my way as I stepped in, and her cheeks were flushed from the heat of the café, and today her hair was braided again but this time it was wrapped at the top of her head in a bun.

Placing my memory of her from the club next to this creature watching me—I would be unable to say they were the same person. That girl had been lovely. Captivating.

This woman was irresistible. I wanted to crawl to her on my knees.

She didn't look surprised to see me. But she didn't look happy either. I didn't know what to make of this resolute creature in front of me.

"Hungry?" she asked, cutting through the thousands of things we could say.

"Yes."

I felt my hunger like a black hole inside of me. My

hunger for her. For that smile in her eye and the glow that suffused her. For a baby, a family. For a place to belong.

"Have a seat at the counter. The eggs and bacon are local—everything else is gross."

"I heard that!" yelled the crusty old woman from yesterday as she walked by.

"Well, it is," said Abby with a shrug.

"Eggs and bacon sound good."

"Have a seat, I'll bring you some coffee."

I sat down and spent the next hour watching her light up the room like she did in the Moonlight Lounge. She had magic, and I didn't know if she even realized how magical she was. Even here in the middle of nowhere, she brought something to the people in this café that had nothing to do with the food. She smiled and touched people's shoulders as she poured their coffee. She looked right into their eyes and said *thank you* and *you're welcome* and *I hope you enjoyed it* with complete sincerity.

It was her dream, the café where everyone came to get what they need, and she was the one pouring it with her coffee.

Finally, I had to turn my back on her before I fell apart. Before I fell to my knees.

At long last she came up to my shoulder, wearing the sweater she wore yesterday, and she had a plate in her hand. An omelette with a side of tomatoes.

"My shift is over," she said. "Can I join you?"

I smiled, though maybe I shouldn't have. This politeness between us was excruciating. I wanted to lean over and whisper in her ear: *remember when you told me to make you come with my mouth?*

"Please," I said, moving my coffee cup and the paper I had been reading. We were pretending something. I just didn't know what it was.

She sat down with a sigh and a slouch and I was immediately concerned for her.

"You all right?" I asked.

"Tired," she said. "My back."

She twisted sideways like there was a kink in her lower back. "Can I—" I asked. My hand hovering over her sweater at the base of her spine.

"Give me a massage? Here in front of God and the Hardt twins?" she asked with a tired laugh.

"I won't if you don't want me to."

"Better not," she said, breaking my heart. I put my hand back on the counter, feeling useless.

She dug into her omelette.

"How long have you been looking for me?"

"Since the moment you left."

Her fork paused on her way to her mouth.

"And if I hadn't walked in here yesterday I would be looking for you until I found you. No matter how long it took."

"To tell me I was safe."

"Yes. And to give you this," I said and pulled from my coat pocket the manila envelope I'd left for her on the bar.

A hundred thousand dollars.

"You told me you loved me," she whispered, her voice in her throat. Her eyes on that envelope. "Remember? The phone call?"

This was one of the things we'd been pretending. Or I had anyway, that the phone call never happened.

"Yes," I said, stiff because I didn't know how to talk about this. "I remember."

"Did you say that because you were scared?" she asked. "Because you thought you were going to die?"

No, I thought. *I said it because I want you. I want that baby. I want us. I want us so badly and I don't know what to do.*

But I couldn't say any of that. Not here.

"Abby," I said, because I couldn't say anything else.

She sighed, low and quiet, and I couldn't stand it anymore, being there and not touching her. I put my hand against her back and she flinched away.

"Don't," she breathed. "I'm not… I can't."

It was like being sliced to pieces. Ribbons. I looked at my body, sure I would see blood, but I was whole.

I stood up. Put my coat on and shoved my hands in

my pockets so I wouldn't put them on her body.

"You're leaving?" she asked, looking up at me with tears in her eyes. As I watched, one trembled past her eyelashes and slipped down her cheek. I touched it before I could stop myself. I popped the bubble of the tear, felt bathed in the salt water of her grief.

The grief I caused just by being near her.

"The money is yours. For you and the baby. No matter what happens. I'm staying out at the Bluebird Motel until you tell me to leave. Do you want me to leave?"

"You're leaving now!" she cried.

I leaned down until we were eye to eye. "I can't do this in here. I can't talk about my feelings while the guy next to us orders the lunch special. Everyone is watching and... I can't, Abby."

She glanced around, seeing what I knew to be true. All eyes were trained on us.

"Do you want me to leave town?" I asked her, because I had to get out of there or lose my mind.

Barely, just barely, she shook her head no.

I turned and left before I made a scene.

Once I was out on the street I put my finger in my mouth, tasting her tear and closing my eyes in pain.

CHAPTER NINETEEN

Jack

AFTER

THE KNOCK ON my door came at sunset. I got up from my bed, putting my old copy of *Too Big To Fail* facedown on the mattress. Old habits and fears made me walk up to the hotel room door sideways, checking the peephole, half expecting to see Bates standing there.

But it was Abby.

I unlocked the door and yanked it open.

"Abby!" I cried, worried and happy all at once. "Is everything okay?"

She stepped in and shut the door behind us, and the hotel room seemed suddenly painfully shabby and way too small. She filled the room with a bright anger. The lamp I had on beside my bed created shadows in all the corners, and she stood in one.

From the front pocket of the baggy sweatshirt she wore she pulled out my manila envelope and put it down on the table. Pushing it with her pale fingers into the middle, like she was making a bet at a casino.

All in.

"I can't stop you from leaving," she said. "But I'm not taking your money so you can do it and feel better about going."

"You need that money," I said, and it must have been the wrong thing because she finally looked at me and she was pissed. Furious. Shaking with anger.

"Don't fucking tell me what I need."

I nodded and held up my hands. "I'm sorry."

"I went to my sister for help that night, after what I—"

"I know what night." I didn't need her to say it out loud. We both needed to put that night behind us.

"And before I could say no, or figure something out for myself, Charlotte was selling her condo and moving into an airport hotel, and I was so used to her doing that. So used to her taking the lead in my life that I let her do it. I let her give me everything she had, because that is what she does.

"And I took half her money from the sale of her condo because that's what I do. But I've spent none of it. Not a penny. Because I can't keep doing that, you know? I can't keep letting her bail me out."

"This money, it's not to bail you out."

"I know. It's to bail *you* out."

I rocked back on my heels.

"I think you want me," she said. "And I think you want this baby. And I think you've spent the last few months just like I have, despite everything that happened, despite being terrified and freaked out—imagining us as a family. And you want that. You really do. Which is why you won't reach for it."

I blinked at her. Stunned at her bravery. Unable to look away from her fierceness.

"You're like the reverse of that dog, you know? The one that hears the bell and drools?"

"Pavlov." The word spilled from my numb lips.

"Right. You want something and you turn your back. And this money is going to make you feel better about turning your back. So," she sighed. "I don't want it."

She stepped toward me and I, feeling like a cornered animal, stepped back. But it didn't dissuade her. She kept coming toward me. So fierce I put my hand out as if to ward her off.

But she, always so foolish. So reckless. She stepped right into my hand, laying her cheek against my palm. Sending sparks up my arm into my blood.

"I want you," she said. "I'm really fucking scared, but I want you."

I wanted her too. I wanted her so badly I could taste it. Like her tear from earlier. Salty and sweet.

And I was scared, but my fear, it was so old. So ingrained.

Do not reach for what you want because the pain, when it comes... it will devastate you. And there is so little of you left. If she leaves. If something happens...

I shook my head. Denying her. Denying us.

"Jack," she breathed and still, I didn't reach for her. Yes, love and faith and belief were a yes and no question, but the living of that answer was complicated.

Dangerous.

She sobbed hard and turned away, shoving me as she went, reaching for the door.

She's leaving. She's leaving!

I put my hand around her waist, stopping her in her tracks. And the door she'd opened I slammed shut with my hand. She jerked against me at the sound and my entire body sighed with relief at the contact.

Her back was to my chest and I felt the shuddering nature of every breath she took, and I knew she felt the wild pounding of my heart against her spine.

"Jack..."

No talking. Talking would ruin everything because I didn't know what to say or how to say it.

I wanted to go back to the way we'd been in my house those three days. Our bodies could figure this out; they'd done it before.

I turned her into my arms, lifting her against me, feeling the swell of her breasts and her belly. I got one wild look at her triumphant eyes and I wanted to warn her. To stop her from feeling like we'd won, because this… us, we might not be winning.

But then it didn't matter. I kissed her like she was everything in the world I needed and was terrified of.

And she kissed me back the same way. Like it was kiss or die.

I carried her, her feet dangling between my calves, to the bed where I tried to be gentle. I tried to careful and caring. I ran my hands over her back and her arms I stopped trying to devour her mouth with mine.

"Stop," she said against my lips.

I jerked back. "What's wrong?"

"You're treating me like I'm going to break."

"I'm—"

"Stop."

"Abby—"

She kissed me, pulling my lower lip into her mouth and biting me.

Fuck, I jerked in her arms and she sucked that lip into her mouth, and I grabbed her. I grabbed her ass in my hand, pulling her so hard against me I felt the bump of her belly and the heat between her legs. Fine, I thought, letting out some of the demons of the last few months. Yes. Good.

Animals.

I pushed her backward onto the bed and followed her down, covering her body with mine, every inch of it. Every bit of her. She curled against me, pushed and pulled her nails against my neck. Her teeth against my tongue.

I yanked the sweatshirt over her head, throwing it over my shoulder. The loose cream tunic she wore beneath it followed.

She wore a blue bra, one of those running ones, and beneath the lower band of it was her tummy. The swell of it. Her creamy skin, pulled taut over her rounded abdomen.

"You're pregnant."

"You knew that," she said.

"I know. I just didn't *know*."

"It surprises me sometimes too," she said. Running her hand over the curve. The blue veins under her skin were fascinating. I could have studied them for hours. "You can touch it," she said. "Touch me."

My hand was shaking. Really shaking as I laid it against her skin. "It's hard," I said. "It's beautiful. You're beautiful."

I crawled off her body, kissing the tops of her breasts. She gasped. I licked her hard nipple through the thick cotton of the bra and she gasped again. So I sucked them through the fabric into my mouth and she arched up off the couch.

I pushed the thick edge of the bra up over her breasts. The red line imprinted on her skin made me ache for her. I kissed the rippled mark the bra left behind, licked the bottom curve of her breasts. The nipples.

She was groaning beneath me. Writhing.

So much more sensitive than she'd been before.

I felt something satisfied and primal uncurl in my chest. The pregnancy did this. I did this. Fuck. I was so hard.

Would she come like this? Could I make her come just like this?

I tongued her nipples until she was crying out.

"Stop," she said, putting her hands over herself, between my mouth and her beautiful body. "Stop. It's too much. Too sensitive."

Conceding, I made my way down her body to the swell of her stomach. The rise of it. I worked off her leggings and underwear, pulled off her shoes until she was lying on that bed naked.

My hand eased between her legs and I found her wet and flush and ripe. My fingers instantly coated in her. Instantly enveloped in her heat.

She whimpered and stretched her arms over her head, her legs splitting open just enough, the slightest invitation, but it was enough and I took it. I was on the floor between her legs, her soft skin under my hands, against my shoulders. I wanted to tear off my clothes so I could feel her everywhere, but this wasn't about me.

This was about her.

My hands slipped up the velvet of her inner thighs, the muscles and tendons there twitching against my touch, like I'd set off some kind of rebellion in her body. I glanced up at her, the swell of her stomach, her breasts, pink and bigger than before, her face, the sharp chin and perfect nose. Her eyes closed. Her mouth open.

I would remember her like this for the rest of my life.

My hands slid higher up her body, around her pregnant belly toward her breasts and she sighed and flinched as I touched her. As I stroked her nipples. Sighs turned to moans and her legs shifted open even further and I smiled.

Yes, my girl. My beautiful responsive girl.

Her pussy was wet and pink and perfect and I put my face against her, breathing her in.

She moaned, her hands touching my hair, my face. I licked her, the pink crease, with the flat of my tongue. Touching as much as I could. Tasting as much as I could. She hitched her hips up, her hands now in fists in my hair. I found the hard bead of her clitoris and she flinched away. I saw her eyes pop open and I stopped.

"That… hurts," she said in a strange voice. Like the sensation was a surprise. But not a bad one.

I leaned back. I'd pull off my skin before I hurt her.

"No, it's just… it's so sensitive," she said with a soft smile.

Her hand left my head to stroke the swell of her stomach, and I realized the pregnancy was changing her. And what a fucking righteous thing that was. What a beautiful force of nature.

"Shhhh." I blew my breath against her like it might make whatever pain I caused feel better. Instead of the tip of my tongue I used the flat of my tongue over and over again, and her body slowly melted against me. I leaned back and ran my fingers through the slick heat between her legs, the touch of my finger against her clitoris made her flinch again but when I slipped a finger inside of her she nearly shot up off the couch.

"Oh my god," she breathed, wide eyed looking at me.

"Too much?" I asked, every muscle still.

"So good. Oh my god." She fell back against the bed and I could feel her, the rising tide of orgasm in the tension of her legs, the fluttering of the muscles inside her body.

I added another finger and she put a hand over her mouth, covering up her cries.

"Do you want more?" I asked.

"Yes, please, it feels so good. I can't…" She looked up at me with wild eyes. "More. Please. I need you to fuck me."

She was wild under my hands, thrumming against my fingers.

"Please, Jack."

I was on some kind of autopilot, unable to resist when she asked like that. When she pleaded me with her eyes, I got up on my knees, pulling her hips closer to the edge of the bed. I unbuckled my belt and undid my pants, half my brain screaming at me to stop.

But I didn't.

And when I slid into her it was the most beautiful feeling I'd ever had in my life.

She cried out, her back bowing. I reached over her to grab the edge of the mattress.

Her legs came up around my hips, holding me against her with surprising strength.

I put every effort into her, pulling myself so far inside my skin so I wouldn't feel how good it was to fuck her.

Every time I sank into her as far as I could she nearly screamed with the pleasure, but when I fucked her fast she shook her head. So I stayed deep, gripping the bed, curling into her with slow, deep, hard thrusts, and she spun out beneath me.

She utterly collapsed.

Crying and twitching, her eyes open and staring unseeing into mine, and I held myself still in the place she seemed to like best, lodged so deep inside her I could feel her heartbeat. *I won't survive this*, I thought, as she came and came and came. *I just can't.*

And when it was over, when she lay beneath me replete and sweating, her skin pink with her pleasure—I still couldn't move.

I remembered those days in my apartment, how it had felt dangerous at first to come. Like it would be committing to a road I'd never return from.

Fuck. Was I ever right.

"Jack," she said, stroking my face. "It's okay. Please. Come."

She sat up to put her arms around me and the shifting of her body around mine was the end of me. I pushed her to the bed and crawled over her, finding the place I liked best, with her ass in my hands and her legs around my waist. I pushed and pulled her across my dick until everything, all of it, was inevitable.

I came in blinding spurts. Painful and ecstatic all at once.

"God, Abby," I breathed, pulling out of her and collapsing at her side. "Are you—"

"Perfect," she said. "I'm totally perfect."

I lifted her onto the bed, pulling the sheets over her, curling my body into hers. And finally I did what I'd been wanting to do all day: I rubbed my hand down her back, digging my fingers into the knots I felt along her spine.

"Oh god," she breathed. "Oh, thank you."

She curled and shifted, sighing and wincing. And I rubbed accordingly. I could spend days like this.

"Jack," she whispered after a long long time.

"Yeah."

"The women in the container…"

I recoiled. Why was she bringing that here? To the bed? But she grabbed my hand, stopping me before I could leave.

"Have you talked to anyone?" she asked.

"I told you."

"Barely," she said. "You barely told me anything."

"You don't want to know that shit, Abby."

"What about the police?"

"They were called that night. The women weren't dropped in the ocean, if that's what you're worried about."

"Yes," she said in a small voice. "But I'm also worried about you."

"You shouldn't be. You have enough going on."

"What about what happened with Lazarus?"

"What are you talking about?"

"You killed a man, Jack. Have you… like, talked to a priest?"

"Abby, baby. Please."

"Okay," she sighed. "I'm sorry. I just…" She shook her head, stopping herself from saying whatever she was going to say.

It took her a while, but she finally relaxed again and I went back to rubbing her spine. When one hand got tired, I moved behind her so I could get to her with my other hand.

After a while I realized she'd stopped moaning and shifting.

She was asleep. Asleep in my arms. In my bed.

I turned off the light and put my head beside hers on the mattress.

I fell asleep too, and dreamt terrible dreams of Abby being locked in a shipping container.

CHAPTER TWENTY

Abby

AFTER

My body was some kind of new beast. That orgasm? That had been some next-level shit right there. And the nap? I mean, I was taking sleep to a new level with this pregnancy, but it was like I'd come and then fallen into a coma.

I wanted a dozen more where those came from. I wanted an endless amount more. I would keep Jack around just for that if I had to.

He was sleeping in the bed as I pulled on my sweatshirt and slipped on my shoes. I couldn't find my underwear, but that was okay.

I thought about what he would say if I told him I wanted him in my life just to give me orgasms. How he would quietly resign himself to that, maybe even manage to be thankful that he got to touch me.

Fuck. That guy.

How was I supposed to be the only one reaching?

The only one risking?

I couldn't, was the answer. I couldn't be the only one doing that. He said he loved me, but he ran away when we talked about it. We had sex, but if I'd told him to leave after I'd come, he would have done it.

He would do anything I asked without asking for anything for himself.

That wasn't sustainable.

Neither was the fact that he hadn't talked to anyone about what happened that night at the Moonlight.

I found the notebook and pen in the small desk in the corner of the room and wrote a note to Jack, and then left him sleeping.

Our future unknown.

In the car I turned on my phone to about twenty texts from my sister. The last said:

You need to get back to me soon or I'm going to call the cops.

I'm fine, I texted her quickly. *I'll text you in ten.*

I'd told her that Jack was here. That he'd given me a bunch of money. I told her that he loved me. And... I might love him.

She did not take any of that news well.

I drove back into town and parked behind the café. I lived in the apartment above it. It was small and smelled like meatloaf, but it was warm and it was quiet and it was mine.

I got myself a glass of water, wrapped myself up in the blanket I'd brought from home. My sister made it for me in some weird fleece craft stage she went through. And in my bedroom I grabbed my phone and texted my sister back.

My sister worried.

Hey, I texted her.

There was no more need for our ridiculous Cheetara Facebook subterfuge. I thought I was so clever when all I'd been was foolish.

Hey, she texted back almost immediately. *Are you all right?*

Fine.

What happened?

We had sex. We had like oh my god sex. Like the best sex ever. Pregnant sex.

Okay. I get the picture.

Get pregnant, sis. I'm telling you…

STOP BEING RIDICULOUS! WHAT IS GOING ON WITH JACK?

I ran my hand over my stomach. I hadn't felt the baby move yet; the doctor and the books I'd read said it would be any day now. And I was anxious for some sign of life past the hormones I'd been flooded with for three months.

I'm a little scared I'm going to have to lock myself in the closet again.

Why? Did he hurt you?

No. Srsly. No. But I can't do this alone, you know? He can't be so scared of wanting something that he wants nothing. I can't live like that.

I'm so worried for you, she wrote.

You have to trust me, I wrote. *Just like I'm trusting you with Jesse.*

It was remarkable that we'd fallen in with brothers. The odds on that had to be legendary.

Jesse is not like Jack, she wrote back fast.

I'm not sure the real Jack is at all like this Jack, I texted back to her. *I think the real Jack is lost in this guy.*

What if you don't like the real Jack? What if the real Jack is a creep?

Impossible, I thought. I'd been falling in love with the real Jack the moment I saw him reading at the bar.

Call it intuition, I texted.

Playing the mother card so soon? she wrote and I could hear her teasing me from across the miles.

I haven't spent your money, I texted. *And I'm not going to. I never should have taken it. I freaked out and fell back on old habits. And worse, I let you fall back on old habits. And I tore apart your life for nothing.*

I don't know, she texted back. *I'm pretty happy with the way things worked out.*

My sister was getting laid on the regular, and she was falling in love and seeing herself in a whole new light, and it was amazing.

I wish I could see you, she texted. *I miss you.*

I miss you too, I texted. *But I just need to do this on my own for a while longer.*

I met Jack outside on the bench in front of the big window. I had a black coffee for him and a tea with milk and sugar for me. I was trying to cut back on the caffeine. And the sugar. It was just too bad that I had constant cravings for McDonald's milkshakes. As he walked up the street toward me I tracked all the differences in him. The black flop of hair over his eyes. The worn blue jeans. He was wearing old beat-up work boots and the same sweater from yesterday.

My body hummed at the sight of him, remembering that orgasm. And my heart… oh, my heart lurched up into my throat with fear that he would not stay. That I would not be enough, and this baby would not be enough to keep him here. That the demons would have him after all.

"Hi!" My grin was wide and undoubtedly goofy, but I was done with secrets. And I was done pretending I didn't feel what I felt. We were adults, and for the first time since we'd met our lives were our own. I would show him how I felt. Because it made me feel good.

"What are you doing?" he asked, coming to stop in front of the bench.

"Waiting for you," I said, because it was the truth on so many levels.

"Everything okay?" he asked. "You left."

"You were sleeping, Jack. I didn't want to wake you. Coffee?"

"Thank you," he said and sat down next to me on the bench, careful to keep distance between us.

That he would deny himself, I had no doubt. But me? Perhaps it was so foolish to think he'd given me all the keys to his kingdom, but it felt that way.

It felt like he was mine.

And I was his.

And he just needed to get comfortable with it. I just needed to let him know it was okay to want something.

"Are you on break?" he asked.

"I'm not working today."

He popped open the small plastic top so he could take a sip of the coffee.

"Do you get used to all this space?" he asked, staring down Main Street toward the mountains in the distance.

"I felt a little claustrophobic at first, which is weird."

"No. I totally get it. So much sky."

We were silent for a long time, each of us taking sips from our cups, and I wondered if he was as nervous as I was. If he'd spent the night working on a speech to give me.

"You told me you loved me," I blurted. I had spent this morning making speeches, but I couldn't remember any of them.

He was very still beside me. Like a statue.

"And I went looking for you, because you said it. Because it mattered to me. Because I wanted it to be true."

I paused, giving him a chance to say that it was true.

But he didn't. He didn't say anything. He sat beside me as silent as ever.

I took a deep breath and launched into the speech I'd written yesterday, wrapped in that blanket, my body made more alive by his touch.

Now, I was losing hope every second.

"I am figuring shit out, Jack. I mean, I'm not great at it, but it's time. Idaho, this place has been a weird gift. Like a silent corner where I could get away from the noise I've been making my whole life. I'm here because for the moment it makes things clear, you know. And I'm… we're having a baby, Jack."

"You are. You are having the baby."

It was like he was taking himself right out of the equation. And I *thought* I knew why he was doing it. But I couldn't keep making up shit about him. I had to *know*.

This was it. This was the moment I thought I could avoid. The one I could pretend wasn't barreling toward me. My optimism took a hit and the breath I sucked in, it shuddered. I looked at him until it hurt. Until I had to look away.

"Do you want… us?" I asked and felt his gaze, intense and sharp on my face. I studied my Styrofoam tea cup like the secrets of the universe were printed on the damp teabag.

He was silent, so silent for so long. And I wondered if I'd gotten this all wrong. If I read his restraint as restraint, because I didn't want to see it as dislike. Or disregard.

Perhaps I'd been filling in the blanks again, with all the wrong things.

How like me. How painfully like me.

"I want you," I said. I laughed at how ridiculous that sounded. How want was not a big enough word. I got to my feet and forced myself to be as much myself as I could. To fill out all my edges. To declare all my intentions, because this was not for him, and not only for this baby.

It was for me.

I had to be clear and I had to be honest for this child, yes. For our future, yes. But I was the builder of that future.

And it was time for honesty.

"I want you," I said. "But I don't need you. And I really don't need your money. I can do this on my own. Here or back in San Francisco or wherever I decide. I can do this."

He looked at me like he knew that. Those resolute

eyes of his made no bones about the fact that I could do whatever I wanted.

"I don't need you, but I want you, Jack. I want you for this baby. And I want you for me."

"Abby," he sighed.

"There's a place for you in the baby's life if that's all you want. We can figure that out. Custody and weekends and whatever it takes. But… this is what I need from you, Jack." I took a deep breath. "If you said what you did on the voicemail because you were scared and you don't think you can really love me. If you don't…desire me, you have to tell me. So that I can stop what I'm feeling. So I can protect my heart." My breath sobbed and I turned away, for just a second. "I don't love you," I said clearly. "But I could. I could love you so easily it's a little terrifying…"

My voice broke.

"And I need you to do some work, Jack. I can't do all the work. I can't come to you all the time. I need you to come to me. And more often, I need you to meet me in the middle.

"And if you think you can do that. If you agree to all that…" I took a deep breath. "I'm going to need you to see a counselor. Or a priest. Someone you can talk to about what you saw. And what you did. Because that will eat at you. It will eat at you until there's nothing left."

We were both looking at our shoes. The constant wind crying and whistling and moaning, a fitting soundtrack for us.

"I live above the café," I said, shuddering my way through this speech because his silence was so difficult. "The stairs are in the back. The door is open. And you can come up anytime, but only if you're honest. Really honest, like I've been with you. Or, you can drive away and we'll just be done. But I need you to come to me, Jack."

I stood there for a second because part of me couldn't believe that he was going to actually let me go upstairs. This decision couldn't be that hard for him.

But clearly it was. Or clearly he was just waiting for me to leave so he could get in his car and drive on.

And the longer I stood there and smeared him with my hope and my belief in this future we could have, the longer I might be putting off the inevitable.

That I'd been wrong about him all along.

He was the cold soulless man he'd been telling me he was all along.

I left without another word.

And he didn't come up.

CHAPTER TWENTY-ONE

Jack

AFTER

I'D LIKE TO say that I followed her up those stairs. That I chased her the way she chased me, never giving her one single moment to doubt my feelings for her.

Or her feelings for me.

But I didn't.

I sat on that bench for a long time. The wind picked up the edge of the stack of napkins she'd been using to insulate her hand against the heat of her Styrofoam cup and blew them off the bench, and I lurched to my feet and grabbed them before they could be carried down the street.

And somehow that was enough, that movement once started, propelled me around the building and up those rickety stairs, so much like the stairs at the Moonlight that it was eerie.

The door wasn't locked and it opened soundlessly under my hand, and I walked into her apartment. The galley kitchen with the double sink and the window looking over the alley. There was a coffee maker and a hot pot and that was about all.

The kitchen opened up into an empty living room with a TV and a couch and a pregnant woman crying on it.

She got up on her feet as soon as she saw me, wiping her tears away angrily, and I could see by the set of her face that she'd started to believe I wasn't coming.

That I would reward her bravery by running away like a coward.

"I don't think I could love you," I said and she flinched back, her mouth slack on a sob. I stepped closer. "I already love you. I didn't leave that voicemail just because I was scared. I left that voicemail because I couldn't die without telling you that."

It was my truth as real as I had, but I wasn't done.

"I loved you from the second you walked over and asked me what I was reading. From the moment you surprised yourself talking about that book, talking about your own intelligence that you've always underestimated. But my love…my love has little value," I told her. "I don't know what I bring to you but the blood on my hands."

"I think," she whispered, "that you have always underestimated your love. And if you love me, let me tell you as an authority." Tears spilled from her eyes and I felt my own welling up in turn. "Your love has tremendous value. Your love might be the most valuable thing I have."

"I have spent so long pushing aside everything I would reach for…"

"I'm right here, Jack," she said, smiling through those tears. "It's not that hard."

Oh, I loved that she called me out. That there was room in all this worry and grief for joy too. I wasn't all tragedy.

The thought was a thunderbolt in my head and I grabbed this woman of joy and glitter and sunshine and I pulled her against me. Held her to me.

And she held me just as hard, showing me with her strength and her intelligence and her beauty just how much value I had.

"What's next?" I asked.

"Sex," she said.

"Yeah?"

She stepped back, leading me from the apartment's living room to the bedroom. The clouds had covered the sun and outside there was a crack of thunder, and it felt like a gift. A rainy day in bed with my woman. I pulled off her shirt, and there, pressed against mine, was the small mound of our baby.

"Our baby," I said. The words sinking in, in a way I'd never let them before. Before, the baby was something I could not have, so I did not think of it.

"Oh my god, our baby!" I gasped again, looking up at Abby with wide eyes. "Jesus. Fuck. What are we going to do?"

She tipped her head back, all that beautiful hair falling down her back, and she laughed and laughed.

"We're going to love this baby, Jack," she said. "It doesn't need to be any more complicated than that. Not right now."

I liked that answer. I liked it a lot.

I walked her backward a few more steps until her legs hit the bed, and she sat down on the edge, and I fell to my knees in front of her, eye level with her stomach.

"Can I?" I asked, lifting my hand to touch her.

She nodded, eyes full again, and I put my hands to her stomach.

"It's hard," I said with a giddy sense of wonder. My hands felt huge against this small miracle, and I put my hands over the width of it, covering it from her hip bone to her hip bone, from the top of the mound to the downward slope of it under the elastic waistband of her pants.

I was, in a way, holding our baby.

Beneath the heel of my left hand I felt a bubble. A flutter. A here-and-then-gone sensation that I thought I might have imagined, except that Abby shrieked and put her hand over mine.

"Did you feel that?" she breathed.

I nodded, incapable of words.

"That was the baby." We stared at each other until I couldn't stand it anymore and I had to hold her in my arms. I stood and got into that bed with her, fully dressed. I kicked off my shoes and pulled her into my arms and I planned on never letting her go.

EPILOGUE

Jack

THE CAR SCREECHED to a stop against the curb, outside of the community college where I taught, which just happened to be two blocks from where Jesse and Charlotte had moved.

We'd all left San Francisco and now we were in Berkley. Far enough away for all of us from the people we'd been.

I got into the passenger seat, but I didn't have my seatbelt on before Jesse was merging back into traffic.

"I think you should let me drive," I said as the driver behind us, whom Jesse had just cut off, laid on the horn.

"No time," Jesse said. He cut across two lanes of traffic to get on the highway.

"We're no good to anyone if you get us killed."

"Stop being so fucking melodramatic," Jesse said.

I didn't say anything. But I smiled.

"What the fuck is so funny?"

"You."

"There are fucking humans coming into the world right now, Jack."

"I'm aware."

My phone dinged and it was a text from Abby.

Where are you? she texted. *Charlotte's asking for Jesse and Maria is asking for you.*

On our way. Five minutes, I texted back.

"I told Charlotte she shouldn't have gone down to the diner today," Jesse said.

"Jesse," I said, clapping his shoulder. He was sweating through his shirt. Poor guy. "Babies come when babies come. It has nothing to do with going down to the diner."

"But she was decorating."

"Because she loves it," I reminded him. "You say one word to Abby like this is somehow her fault, and I will gut you like a fish."

Jesse's scowl broke reluctantly into a smile. "Some talk from an economics nerd."

Right. And considering my MMA champion brother could snap me like a twig was not worth mentioning. But he slowed down and we made it to the hospital in one piece.

"Go," I said as we screeched to a stop in front of the emergency room. "I'll park."

"Thank you," Jesse said and unbuckled his seat belt. He was halfway out the door when he stopped and looked back at me. "Is it supposed to feel like this?"

"Like you want to cry and shit your pants at the same time?"

He nodded.

"Yes. That is exactly the right feeling for a husband when his wife is in labor with their first baby."

He scratched at his chest, the area over his heart, and I knew that feeling too, had felt it twice now. The itch of the heart as it began its expansion, preparing itself for more love.

"Am I going to fuck this up?" he whispered.

"No," I said quickly, putting my hand on his shoulder again. The guy was nervous flop sweating like a fucking champ. "But if you do, you've got backup. We're all here, Jesse."

Abby, Charlotte, me and Jesse.

We were the family now. The support. And we were stronger than I could have ever dreamed.

My brother ran off, looking like a damp berserker, and I parked and found myself down familiar hallways to the delivery section of the hospital. I rounded the family waiting room corner and there was my Maria, sitting at a table coloring.

She wore head to toe orange, because that was her favorite color right now and there was no talking her out of a full embracing of something she loved.

My daughter lived her life like I wished I could live mine. Full tilt. All in. I watched her with her black pigtails and her tongue between her lips as she went to town on some waiting room coloring book like it was just the very best thing.

We'd named her after my mother.

It had been Abby's idea, and I was still destroyed by love for her.

"Hey!" It was Abby behind me and I turned, lifting my arm over her shoulder in what had become a reflex. "You're here."

"I am." I leaned over to kiss her cheek and she handed the baby to me. Our baby. Oscar. Three months old. "How is Char?"

"A trooper."

"How are you?" I asked her, kissing her again. And again. She looked tired, we both did. Babies, man. But she was still the brightest thing for miles.

"Excited," she said with happy eyes. There really wasn't enough family for Abby. "But," she said, "not nearly as excited as Maria."

That wasn't a surprise either.

"Sweet girl!" I said, and Maria finally looked up from her drawings.

"Hey daddy!" I went to her and sat down in the other uncomfortable plastic chair so I could talk to her while she colored. Oscar slept in my arms and Abby was in and out of Charlotte's delivery room for the next few hours. I settled into the wait, happy in the moment. More content with my numb ass and my sleepy children than I would have dreamed possible.

Abby came in late and sat down beside me. "Shouldn't be long now," she whispered.

"You're not staying in the room?" My wife and her twin had only gotten closer in the last few years. I really couldn't believe it possible, but working on the café together and having children and marrying my brother and me… well, they were tight.

"No," she said smothering a yawn. "It's for them."

Just like it had been for us. I kissed her hand, handed Oscar over to be fed, and went back to my extended game of Go Fish.

Around midnight, my brother emerged. Eyes red from crying. Exhausted but lit up at the same time, and my soul tripped over at the sight of that happiness. Like one more weight of my three years in the darkness had been cast off.

All of us stood: Abby, Maria, and me, a unit buoyed on excitement and hope and family.

"Boys," Jesse said. "Twin boys."

After so long with so little, our lives were exploding with so much.

Hey!

Thank you so much for reading Baby, Come Back. I hope you enjoyed Abby and Jack! Please consider leaving a review – reviews, good or bad, are super important to authors and readers!

And if you liked this book and want some more of my stuff – join my newsletter – I've got exciting news about a new series coming out soon and you don't want to miss it!

www.molly-okeefe.com/subscribe

For more fun join my Facebook Group O'Keefe's Keepers – for awesome author takeovers, free books and special giveaways:

facebook.com/groups/1657059327869189

Curious about Jesse and Charlotte – turn the page for a sneak peek of their story.

http://amzn.to/2npi6Nk

BAD NEIGHBOR
Chapter 1

Charlotte

IN THE END, the futon was my downfall.

It wasn't having my sister leave for parts unknown.

Or giving her most of my money.

Or moving out of the condo I loved so much, only to move to this shithole apartment, where there was a good chance I was going to get knifed before I even got my stuff in the door.

So far, none of that had made me so much as swear. Much less cry. Or scream.

That stuff is just my life. It's the shit that happens to me. Part of being a twin to my sister.

But this futon…

This futon was a punishment from God. It was the universe laughing at me.

It was stuck in the door of my new apartment,

folded up like a taco. An immoveable, three-thousand-pound taco.

And it wasn't moving.

This is just what you get for not hiring movers. Or having a boyfriend. Or anyone really, who could help move a girl with five boxes, three garbage bags, and a futon mattress to her name.

Oh, and several thousand dollars in computer and drafting equipment. All sitting safely in the corner of my apartment. I moved Izzy in first (yes, I named my system. It seemed only right, considering how much time I spend with her) and threw a sheet over her. Paranoid about this new neighborhood, I locked up between trips to my rental truck to get the rest of my stuff. Which was now all sitting behind me on the cracked cement walkway.

Except for the current bane of my existence.

The futon.

Which, I'd like to point out, I got out of the back of the truck, dragged down the path from the parking garage to this point, actually folded it up like a taco and got it halfway through the door.

But now my shaky-exhausted-unused-to-this-amount-of-work (any kind of work actually that doesn't involve a mouse, a pencil or a stylus) muscles had given up.

And to add insult to injury, my hair was getting in

on the joke, by pulling out of my hair elastic and headband to pop up in white-blond corkscrews and fall into my face. It was sticking to my neck.

It was making me crazy.

Everything. Every single thing was making me crazy. After two weeks of keeping my shit together I was going to lose it. Right here.

Stop. Charlotte, you can do this

I gave myself a little pep talk and swallowed down the primal scream of "WHAT THE FUCK HAS HAPPENED TO MY LIFE!"

"Come on," I muttered and put my back up against the futon. I put my back against it and pushed. And got nothing. Got nowhere.

Exhausted, my legs buckled and I barely caught myself against the futon before landing flat on my butt.

I turned and pushed my face and hands against the futon, stretched my legs out behind me, and pushed with all my not-inconsiderable weight.

Suddenly, it bent sideways, throwing me nearly into the wall, and then lodged itself, half in my door and half against the metal staircase leading up to the second floor of the apartment building.

Nope. No. I wasn't going to cry. Not over this.

I just needed help.

And if the thought of actually having to talk to a human to make that help happen, seemed to me to be worse than the futon nightmare, that was just my damage.

You have to get over this, my sister used to tell me. *The world is full of people. No one lives a completely people-free life.*

The only people I used to need were my sister, the girl who made my afternoon coffee at the coffee shop on my old corner, and the fantasy of one of the guys down at the organic fruit stand near where I used to live.

But now they were all gone.

I needed new people.

And the fact that I had to find those people here, at Shady Oaks, this end-of-the-road place... well, it made me want to howl.

The small outdoor courtyard I was currently trapped in was empty. The three stories of balcony loomed over my head, the chipped paint a kind of nondescript beige. The pool in the middle—filled with a half-foot of last year's dried-up leaves and a few hundred cigarette butts—had a few busted-up lawn chairs sitting around its edge, but no one was sitting in them. The laundry area beneath the staircase directly across the courtyard from me was dark and quiet.

My new apartment was beneath the other corner stairway, a weird little shadowy enclave of privacy that the superintendent said leaked—but only when it rained.

The superintendent was more funny *sob*, than funny *ha ha*, if you asked me.

I'd never actually met the super, if you could believe that. Everything was done through email. Which at the time had seemed ideal. Now it seemed…sketchy.

Shady Oaks was a ghost town.

Normally I'd love that. But today, today I just needed a little help. Today I needed a flesh-and-blood person.

And of course there was no one.

I gave myself exactly a three count of pity. That was it. That was all I got.

One.

Two.

"What's going on?" a voice asked. A male voice. And I leaned away from the wall and looked around my futon mattress to see a … guy.

Like a guy guy. A hot guy.

A man, really.

A very sweaty man. His frayed gray tee shirt where it stretched across his shoulders was black with sweat, and it poured down his face. He was my height, maybe a few inches taller. Which in the world of dudes made him kind of short. But he was thick and square, giving the impression that he was taller than he was. And bigger.

Did I say big?

While I watched, he lifted the bottom edge of his shirt and wiped his forehead, revealing that even his six-pack abs were sweating.

"You gonna move this thing?" he asked, scowling at me while I stared at his abs.

I blew a curl out of my face and tried for my best cheerful tone. I even smiled.

"Trying to. But I think the futon likes it here."

"I can't get into my apartment," he said. Ignoring my joke, he pointed at the door next to mine, the door he couldn't get to past the futon barricade.

"Oh," I said, inanely, trying not to stare at his sweat or his body. "We're neighbors."

"Yeah. What are you doing with the futon?"

"Well, you're welcome to try and reason with it, but I've found it very disagreeable—"

"You moving it in or out?" he asked. My charm completely not charming to him.

"In—"

With one hand—*one hand*—he shoved the futon into my apartment. After it squeezed through the door it flopped open in the middle of my white-tiled kitchen.

I leaned into my doorway.

"Wow," was all I could say.

"You want it there?" he asked.

"In my kitchen?" I laughed. "While I can appreciate the commute for coffee—"

Sweaty grumpy guy had dark brown eyes—Pantone color 0937 TCX, if I was being exact—set wide in a flushed face, and I only got a glimpse of them before he was inside my apartment.

Without asking, he just stomped right in.

"Wait…what!"

"Bedroom?" he asked.

I blinked at him, thinking of my livelihood under the sheet in the corner, and if he tried to rob me I wouldn't be able to stop him.

I wouldn't be able to stop him from do-ing…anything.

And I'd had that fantasy about the guys at the fruit stand locking me inside the store with all of them. But this was not that.

This was Shady Oaks, and a burly stranger just walking into my apartment like he had that kind of right.

"Do you want this in your bedroom?" He said it slowly, like I was an idiot.

"You don't have to do this."

"You can't do it." His eyes skated across my body, taking in my paint-splattered overalls and the hot pink tank top I wore underneath it.

He couldn't see that my tank top had Big Bird on it.

But he looked at me like he knew.

He looked at me like I had a sign that said *185-pound weakling* on it.

"I'm putting it in your bedroom."

And he took the futon by the corner, like the hand of a misbehaving child, and dragged it through my shabby kitchen, past the living room with its bank of barred windows, and then into my bedroom. I followed but stopped in the living room by the sheet-covered Izzy, as if to keep her calm, or to stand in his way in case he tried to touch her.

I could just see the shadow of him in my bedroom as he all but tossed my futon onto the floor.

Funny how he was doing a nice thing, but still I managed to feel both threatened and insulted.

Deep breath, Charlotte, I told myself. *Deep breath.*

He was out a second later, standing in the doorway of my bedroom, thick and square. His damp shirt clung to every muscle. And he had...he had a lot of muscles. Thick round knobs of them. Lean, hard planes of them. He was made of muscles.

He'd been running, or working out or something. He wore running shoes and athletic shorts that were frayed in the same well-used way his shirt was. White earbuds had been tucked into the waistband of his shorts, and dangled down by his...well. Shorts.

His black hair was buzzcut short, down practically

to his scalp. And his face, now that the flush was gone and the sweat had slowed down, looked like it had recently taken a beating. His eye was dark and his lip had a cut. His nose looked like it had been broken a few times.

He carried himself like a guy who lived in his whole body. Like every molecule was under his control. I lived in exactly 12% of my body. I wasn't even sure what my hair was doing.

"You done?" he asked.

"Moving?"

"Staring."

All the blood in my body roared to my face. My stomach curled into a ball like a wounded hedgehog trying to protect itself from further harm.

"Thank you," I said, staring intently at the edge of a tile in my kitchen. It was chipped, the white enamel long gone. "That was nice of you to help."

"No big deal." He stepped into the living room and I went back against the wall, giving him a wide, wide berth. Wanting to keep as much distance between us as I could.

He stopped. "What are you doing?"

"Nothing."

"You think I'm going to hurt you?"

"I'm not sure what you're going to do."

He made a grunting noise and stood there like he

was waiting for me to look at him, but I did not. I burned under his gaze and fussed with my sheet, wishing Izzy was set up so I could just work, instead of… this.

Instead of being human with humans.

And then he was gone. Leaving behind the smell of man. And sweat. And it was not a bad smell. It was just different, and it did not belong in my space.

I folded forward at the waist, sucking in a breath.

Jeez. Wow.

That dude was potent.

And I was pretty much an idiot.

I walked into the bedroom and used all of my strength to slide the futon out of the middle of the room and against the wall. There was another thump in the living room, and I realized with my heart in my throat that I'd left my door open. I ran out only to find my sheet still over Izzy, but the rest of my stuff had been brought in.

Two big boxes and the garbage bags.

He'd moved the rest of my stuff in and then he left.

That was…nice.

Unexpected and nice.

Neighborly, even.

I thought about knocking on his door to say thank you. It was what I should do. It was the right thing to do. Neighborly. It was what my sister would have done.

My sister would have gone over and thanked him and then probably screwed him.

But I was not that person. I was the opposite of that person.

Silently, like he could hear me—and maybe he could, I had no idea how thick these walls were—I stepped to my door and then shut it.

And then locked it

And chained it.

Taking a deep breath, I turned and looked at my new home, with its chipped tile and the barred windows. The bare lightbulbs hanging from the ceiling. Outside, there was a siren and a dog barking.

Next door, my neighbor turned on his stereo, answering the question regarding how thick my walls were. Paper thin.

For a moment the grief and the panic and fear were overwhelming. Tears burned behind my eyes and I couldn't take a deep breath. But I pushed the panic back. Smothered it. Just set it aside like a bag I didn't want to carry anymore. I had so many of those kinds of bags, all along the edges of my life.

I closed my eyes and searched for calm.

Deep breath, Charlotte. This is not so bad. This is not forever. This is not permanent. This place is not your world.

I opened my eyes and took in my new home again,

with my rose-colored glasses fully in place.

It wasn't so bad here. The hardwood floors in the living room and bedroom were nice. A coat of paint. Some curtains to hide the bars. My coffee pot. Izzy up and humming in the corner.

It would feel like home. It would.

I could ignore the neighbor. I was good at ignoring actual humans.

As bad as this place was, and it was bad, I had to remind myself that it was actually perfect.

Because no one—even if they were looking—would find me here.

And my sister was okay. She was safe.

Which was all that mattered.

Pick up Bad Neighbor

http://amzn.to/2npi6Nk

70716463R00171

Made in the USA
San Bernardino, CA
05 March 2018